Little Women

by

LOUISA MAY ALCOTT

ESPECIALLY EDITED FOR

THE GOLDEN PICTURE CLASSICS
by Emma Gelders Sterne

ILLUSTRATED BY

Julian Paul

PUBLICITY PRODUCTS • LONDON

Contents

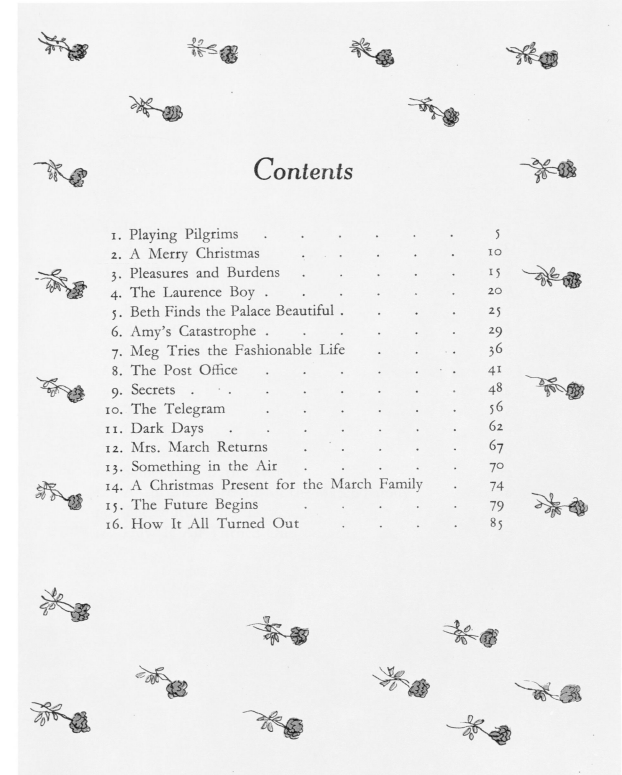

CHAPTER 1

Playing Pilgrims

"CHRISTMAS won't be Christmas without any presents," grumbled Jo, lying on the rug in front of the blazing hearth. The firelight shone on her dark hair and cast shadows on her thin, brown face. She kicked up her heels in a most unladylike fashion. But fifteen-year-old Josephine March cared nothing about being ladylike. She had always regretted not being born a boy and now, more than ever, when the Civil War was raging in the land.

"You know the reason Mother proposed not having any presents this Christmas," sighed Meg, the oldest of the four March girls. "She thinks we ought not to spend money for pleasure when our men are suffering so in the Army. We can't do much, but we ought to make what little sacrifices we can."

"It's so dreadful to be poor," little Amy pouted. "I don't think it's fair for some girls to have plenty of pretty things and others nothing at all."

"We've got Father and Mother and each other," said Beth shyly.

"We haven't got Father," said Jo, thinking of their father far away where the fighting was. "And I don't think the little we'd spend on Christmas will do any good to the soldiers. I agree not to expect anything from Mother or from you girls, but we've each got a dollar, and I do want to buy that book of adventure tales I've wanted so long."

"I had planned to spend mine for new music," sighed Beth.

"And I need drawing pencils most awfully!" Amy exclaimed.

"Let's each buy what we want and have a little fun. I'm sure we work hard enough to earn it," cried Jo.

Meg nodded. "I know I do—teaching those tiresome King children all day."

"You don't have half as hard a time being a governess as I do shut up with fussy old Aunt March for hours," Jo answered.

"I do think helping Hannah with the housework and washing dishes is the worst work in the world," sighed Beth. "My hands get so stiff I can scarcely practice on the piano."

"I don't believe any of you suffer as I do." Twelve-year-old Amy shook her yellow curls in despair. "You don't have to go to school with girls who laugh at your patched dresses and label your father if he isn't rich."

"If you mean *libel*, I'd say so, and not talk about *labels* as if Father were a pickle bottle," Jo laughed.

"At least I don't use slang words and lie on the floor like a tomboy," returned Amy with dignity.

Jo immediately sat up, put her hands in her pockets, and began to whistle. "Don't, Jo," Meg pleaded. "You should remember you are a young lady."

"I'm not. If putting up my hair makes me one, I'll wear it down till I'm twenty." Jo pulled off her net and let her chestnut mane fall over her shoulders. "I hate to think I've got to grow up and be as prim as a China aster. I like boys' games, and I'm dying to go and fight with Papa. But I can only stay home and knit like a poky old woman!"

As she jerked out her knitting needles and began to work on a blue woollen army sock, the clock struck six. Beth jumped up and put her mother's house slippers by the hearth to warm. Somehow the sight of the old shoes had a good effect upon the girls.

Meg stopped lecturing; Amy got out of the easy chair and plumped the pillows without being told; Jo held the slippers nearer the blaze.

"They are quite worn out," she said. "Marmee must have some new ones."

"I thought I'd get her some with my dollar," said Beth.

"No, I shall!" cried Amy.

"Let's each get her something for Christmas," suggested Beth.

"Capital!" exclaimed Jo. "What shall we get?"

"Gloves," said Meg, looking at her own pretty hands.

"The slippers from me," said Jo.

"Some handkerchiefs, all hemmed," said Beth, who at thirteen was an accomplished needlewoman.

"I'll get a little bottle of cologne," said Amy. "She likes it, and it won't cost much, so I'll still have some left to buy my pencils."

"We'll have to go shopping tomorrow," said Jo, marching up and down. "Let Marmee think we're getting things for ourselves. We'll put the surprises on the breakfast table Christmas morning. With Marmee's presents and our play, it will be a merry Christmas after all!"

On holidays and birthdays the girls often gave plays which Jo wrote and directed. "We ought to rehearse," said Meg, who loved to act the romantic heroines in a white cheesecloth costume and gold-paper jewellery.

"I don't see how Jo can write such splendid things as *The Witch's Curse*," Beth said. "She's a regular Shakespeare."

"Not quite," replied Jo modestly. "I'd like to try *Macbeth*, if we only had a trap door for Banquo. I always wanted to do the killing part. 'It that a dagger I see before me?' " she recited, clutching at the air.

"No, it's the toasting fork with Marmee's slipper on it," cried Meg amid a general burst of laughter.

"Glad to find you so merry, my girls," said a cheery voice at the door, and Mrs. March came into the room.

Beth took her mother's grey cloak and bonnet. Amy knelt to pull off the snowy outdoor shoes and put on the well-toasted slippers. Meg flew about arranging the tea table. Jo brought in wood and drew up chairs, dropping and clattering everything she touched.

As they gathered about the table, Mrs. March said, "I've got a treat for you after supper."

A quick, bright smile went round like a streak of sunshine. Beth clapped her hands, and Jo tossed her napkin in the air, crying, "A letter! A letter from Father!"

"Yes, a nice, long letter. He sends loving wishes for Christmas and a special message to you girls."

"I think it was splendid of Father to go as a chaplain when he was too old to fight," said Meg warmly.

"Don't I wish I could be with him—as a drummer or even a nurse," groaned Jo, as they drew near the fire to hear the letter.

It was a cheerful, hopeful letter filled with descriptions of camp life, marches, and military news. Only at the end did the father's heart overflow with love and longing for his family at home:

I know my girls will be loving children and will do their duty faithfully so when I come back home I may be prouder than ever of my little women.

Mrs. March folded the letter soberly. "Do you remember how you used to play Pilgrim's Progress when you were younger? You'd travel with bundles on your backs from the cellar, which was the pilgrim's City of Destruction, up, up—"

"To the top floor where our burdens fell off and tumbled downstairs. Then we'd go on with light hearts—"

"'Till we came out on the flat roof that was Christian's Celestial City. We'd look down on the treetops and flowers and sing for joy!'"

"And have cake and milk," Amy added. "If twelve years old wasn't too grown-up, I'd like to play it over again."

"We are never too old to play Pilgrim's Progress," her mother answered. "We play it all the time in one way or another. Our burdens are here, our road is before us. The longing for goodness and happiness guides us through troubles to the Celestial City. Suppose my pilgrims begin —not in play but in earnest—till Father comes home. Each of you has her burden —Meg, her work; Jo, her temper; Amy, her selfishness. . ."

"Beth hasn't any," Jo interrupted.

"Yes, I have," sighed Beth. "Mine is dishes and envying girls with nice pianos and being afraid of people. Before you came home, Marmee, we were in the Slough of Despond."

"And you pulled us out, as Help did in Bunyan's book," said Jo, delighted with her mother's plan. "We ought to have our roll of directions, like Christian. What shall we do about that?"

"Look under your pillows on Christmas morning," answered Mrs. March.

CHAPTER 2

A Merry Christmas

Jo was the first to wake in the grey dawn of Christmas morning. She slipped her hand under her pillow and drew out a little crimson-covered book. It was that beautiful old story of the best life ever lived, and Jo felt it was a true guidebook for any pilgrim.

Meg's book was bound in green, Beth's was dove-coloured, and Amy's, blue. Their mother had written a few words inside each which made the presents very precious, and the girls resolved to read a few passages every day.

When the east grew rosy with the coming day, Jo and Meg put aside the books

and ran downstairs. Hannah was there before them, building up the kitchen fire.

"Merry Christmas, Hannah! Where's Marmee?" Meg asked.

"Goodness only knows. Some boy came a-beggin', and your ma went straight off to see what was needed. There never was such a woman for givin' away vittles and clothes and good firewood," grumbled Hannah. "And me all ready to fry the cakes for Christmas breakfast!"

"Fry away," said Meg. "I'm sure she'll be back soon."

The presents for Mrs. March had been hidden under the sofa in a basket. Meg peeped inside to be sure that everything was ready. "Why, where is Amy's bottle of cologne?" she asked.

"She took it out a minute ago and went off to put a ribbon on it or some such notion," Hannah answered.

"There's Marmee at the door! Hide the basket!" cried Jo.

But it was only Amy who came in. She wore her cloak and hood and was thoroughly out of breath.

"Where have you been and what are you hiding behind you?" asked Meg.

"Don't laugh at me. I only went to change the little bottle for a big one, and I gave *all* my money to get it."

Another bang of the street door sent the basket under the sofa and the girls to the table, eager for the festive breakfast.

"Merry Christmas, Marmee! Thank you for our books. We mean to read some every day," they cried out in a chorus. "Breakfast is ready!"

"Merry Christmas, my dears. But I want to say one word before we sit down. Not far away from here lies a poor woman with a little newborn baby. Five children are huddled into one bed to keep from freezing, for they have no fire. The oldest boy came to tell me. My girls, will you give them your breakfast as a Christmas present?"

There was a moment's silence broken by Beth. "May we go and help carry the things?" The others began piling the steaming, fragrant buckwheat cakes and bread into a basket. Hannah was already gathering firewood in her arms.

They were soon ready, and the procession set out through back streets to the bare, miserable room that was the Hummel family's home.

"Ach, it is good angels come to us," murmured Mrs. Hummel.

"Funny angels in boots and mittens and cold noses," answered Jo as she turned to help Hannah make a fire.

That was a very happy breakfast, and when they went home to their own bread and milk, there were not in all the town four merrier people than the hungry March girls who had given away their Christmas breakfast. Meg slipped ahead and set out the presents on the table. Beth ran to the piano and played her gayest march.

"Open the door, Amy! Three cheers for Marmee!" cried Jo, as Meg escorted their mother to the table.

Mrs. March smiled with her eyes full of tears as she examined her presents. The slippers went on at once; a new handkerchief, well scented with Amy's cologne, was slipped into her pocket; and the new gloves were pronounced a perfect fit.

By the time breakfast was over, the morning was almost gone and the rest of the day was devoted to preparation for the play. Scenery was made from cardboard, gorgeous robes from old cotton and silver paper. Armour was covered with bits of tin garnered from the pickle factory. The stage was set in the big spare bedroom, and the folding bed let down to serve as seating space for the audience.

Jo played the hero and any other men's parts that were needed, wearing the russet leather boots that had been given her by a friend who knew a lady who knew an actor. The boots, together with an old sword and a doublet once used by an artist, were Jo's chief treasures and appeared on all such occasions.

At dusk, a dozen girls from the neighbourhood piled on the bed and sat before the chintz curtain in a most flattering state of expectancy. Behind the curtain there was a good deal of whispering and a giggle or two from Amy. At last a bell sounded, the curtains flew apart, and *The Witch's Curse: An Operatic Tragedy* began.

Thrilling scenes followed, one by one. A witch's cave was replaced by a towering castle which unfortunately tottered and fell with a crash that cut short the love scene of Act II. The third act was played in the castle hall where the villain drank from the poison cup prepared for the hero, and, after a good deal of clutching and stamping, fell flat and died. A fourth and fifth act followed in which all ended happily for the two lovers, Roderigo and the fair Zara.

Tumultuous applause ended only when the folding bed began slowly to close on the audience. The actors came to the rescue, and all were taken out, laughing and unhurt. The excitement had hardly subsided when Hannah appeared, with "Mrs. March's compliments and would the ladies walk down to supper."

This was a surprise even to the actors, and when they saw the table, they looked at one another in silent amazement. There was real ice cream—two great bowls of it, pink and white—and cake and fruit and handsome French bonbons. And in the middle of the table, four great bouquets of hothouse flowers!

"Is it fairies?" gasped Amy.

"It's Santa Claus," said Beth.

"Aunt March?" guessed Jo.

"All wrong. Old Mr. Laurence sent the supper," replied their mother.

"The Laurence boy's grandfather? What in the world—we don't even know him!" exclaimed Meg.

"You mean the people who live in the big house next door?" asked one of the guests. "My mother says he's very proud and doesn't like to mix with the neighbours. He keeps his grandson shut up when he isn't walking or riding with his tutor, and makes him study dreadfully hard."

Mrs. March explained. "Hannah told his gardener about your breakfast party. Mr. Laurence sent me a nice note this afternoon, saying he hoped I would allow him to express his friendly feeling toward my children by sending a few trifles in honour of the day. So you have a little feast to make up for your bread-and-milk breakfast."

"That boy put it into his head. I know he did!" cried Jo. "He's a capital fellow, and I wish we could get acquainted. I spoke to him once when Beth's cat jumped over the garden hedge. He looks as if he'd like to know us, but he's bashful, and Meg is so prim she won't let me make friends with him. I mean to know him someday, though, for he needs fun. I'm sure he does," declared Jo, as the plates went round, and the ice cream began to melt out of sight.

CHAPTER 3

Pleasures and Burdens

"Jo! Jo! Where are you?" cried Meg, at the foot of the garret stairs.

"Up here!" answered Jo's voice from above. Meg found her on an old sofa eating russet apples and crying over a sad story. This was Jo's favourite refuge. Here she loved to retire to enjoy the quiet and the society of a pet rat who lived nearby, to read or to write page after page of her own "book."

As Meg appeared, Scrabble, the rat, whisked off, and Jo looked up to hear the news.

"We've a regular note of invitation from Mrs. Gardiner for a party tomorrow night: *Mrs. Gardiner would be happy to see Miss March and Miss Josephine at a little dance on New Year's Eve*. Marmee is willing we should go. Now, what shall we wear?"

"What's the use of asking that?" mumbled Jo, taking a bite of apple. "You know we'll wear our poplins because we haven't anything else. Yours is as good as new, but there's that awful scorched spot in the back of mine where I burnt it."

"You must sit still all you can and keep your back out of sight," Meg declared firmly. "I shall have a new ribbon for my hair, and Marmee will lend me her little pearl pin. My new slippers are lovely, and my gloves will do."

On New Year's Eve, Mrs. March and the two younger girls stood at the door watching Meg and Jo depart for the dance, with Hannah to escort them to the door. They looked very nice in spite of a few mishaps—Meg in silvery grey with a blue velvet snood, lace frills, and the pearl pin; Jo in maroon with a stiff linen collar, and a white chrysanthemum as her only ornament. No matter that Meg's high-heeled slippers were very tight and hurt her, or that Jo's nineteen hairpins all seemed to be sticking straight into her head!

"Is my sash right?" asked Meg, as she turned from the looking glass in Mrs. Gardiner's dressing room. "Now then, Jo, don't forget to keep the back of your dress out of sight, and *do* act ladylike."

Down they went, feeling a little timid, for they seldom went to parties. Meg was asked to dance at once and went tripping away on her high heels so briskly that no one would have guessed the pain their wearer suffered. Jo felt a little forlorn left alone, but when she saw a red-headed youth coming toward her, she fled into a curtained recess, intending to watch in peace. Unfortunately, another bashful person had chosen the same refuge, for as the curtain fell behind her, she found herself face to face with the Laurence boy!

"I didn't know anyone was here!" stammered Jo, preparing to back out as hastily as she had come in.

The tall, black-eyed boy laughed. "Don't mind me; stay if you like. I only came in here because I don't know many people and felt rather strange."

"So did I," said Jo. "Don't go away, please, unless you'd rather."

They stood for a moment in awkward silence. Then Jo said primly, "I think I've had the pleasure of seeing you before. You live near us, don't you?"

"Next door." The boy laughed outright, for Jo's prim manner was rather funny and so unlike her everyday self. "How is your cat, Miss March?"

"Nicely, thank you, Mr. Laurence. But I'm not Miss March. I'm only Jo."

"And I'm not Mr. Laurence. I'm only Laurie. My name is Theodore, but I don't like it, so people call me Laurie."

"Mine's Josephine, and I hate it."

"Do you like to dance, Miss Jo?" he asked, looking as if he thought the name suited her.

"I like it well enough, but not tonight. Don't you dance?"

"Sometimes. But I've been abroad a good many years, and I don't know how they do things here."

"Abroad!" cried Jo. "Tell me about it. Did you go to Paris?"

"Spent last winter there. I like Italy best, though. I mean to live there someday and enjoy myself in my own way—Listen to that splendid polka they're playing! Don't you want to try it?"

"Can't. I told Meg—that's my sister, Margaret—I wouldn't, because—"

"Because what?" Laurie asked, as Jo stopped short.

"Well, I have a bad trick of standing before the fire, and I burned my frock. Meg told me to keep still so the scorched spot wouldn't show. You may laugh if you want to. It's funny, I know."

But Laurie didn't laugh. "Never mind," he said. "There's a long hall beyond here. We can dance grandly there, and no one will see us."

The hall was empty; Laurie danced well and taught Jo a new step, so that she thoroughly enjoyed herself. When the music stopped, they sat on the stairs and talked until just before supper when Meg appeared in search of her sister.

Jo followed her to a small room, and Meg sank down on the sofa, holding her foot and looking pale. "I've turned my ankle in these stupid slippers. It aches terribly. I don't know how I'm ever going to get home."

"Can I help you?" Laurie's friendly voice said, coming to the doorway with a cup of coffee in each hand.

"It's nothing—I turned my foot a little," Meg said hurriedly.

Laurie immediately offered his grandfather's carriage to take them home.

So after a gay supper together in the little side room, they rolled away in the closed carriage feeling very festive and elegant. Laurie rode on the box with the coachman so Meg could keep her foot up.

Meg's foot was quite recovered the morning after the party, but she woke up out of sorts. It did seem hard to have to take up work again after the gay holiday.

"I wish it was Christmas or New Year's all the time," she sighed.

"Don't let's grumble, but shoulder our burdens like pilgrims and trudge along," said Jo. "I'm sure Aunt March is a regular Old Man of the Sea to me, but I suppose when I've learned to carry her without complaining, she'll tumble off or get so light I shan't mind her."

But Beth was headachy, and Amy couldn't remember what nine times twelve was, and Meg was still cross at breakfast.

She was fond of luxury, and her chief trouble was poverty. When she turned sixteen, she had begged to be allowed to work and had found a place as nursery governess. But at her work, she saw every day the kind of life she fancied. She tried not to be envious, but she could not help contrasting her shabby dresses and work-aday world with the fine clothes and parties of the lively, older girls in the King household.

Jo had happened to suit their wealthy old great-aunt, who was lame and needed a companion. This sort of work did not suit Jo at all, but to everyone's surprise, she got on remarkably well with her tempestuous relative.

The real compensation for the hard work at Aunt March's was a large library of fine books. The moment the old lady took her nap, Jo hurried to the dim, unused room that had been left to dust and spiders since old Mr. March had died. Curling up in the easy chair, the young bookworm devoured poetry, romance, history, and travels until her aunt's shrill voice called, "Josyphine! Josyphine!" and the parrot echoed the cry until the big house rang with Jo's name.

Aunt March and the Kings were burdens to be borne, surely, and the girls did not look forward to beginning again after the holidays.

"If Marmee shook her fist instead of throwing a kiss, it would serve us right," said Jo, "for more ungrateful wretches than we are were never seen. We are a set of rascals this morning. Too much holiday, I fear."

"Call yourself any names you like. I am neither a rascal nor a wretch, and I don't choose to be called so," snapped Meg.

"You're a mistreated princess today. Poor dear, wait till I make my fortune, and you shall ride in carriages and eat ice cream and dance in high-heeled slippers with red-headed boys every day."

"How ridiculous you are, Jo!" laughed Meg at Jo's nonsense. But Jo gave her an encouraging pat on the shoulder, and they went their separate roads, each hugging her little warm turnover.

Hannah stalked in and laid two hot turnovers on the table. These turnovers were an institution in the household. The girls called them "muffs," for they had no others, and found the hot pies very comforting to their hands on cold mornings. Hannah never forgot them, no matter how busy or grumpy she might be.

"Now then, Meg!" Jo tramped out the door, feeling that the pilgrims were not carrying their burdens as well as they might. Meg followed in silence, but before turning the corner, they looked back. As always, there was their mother at the window, nodding and smiling and waving her hand to them. Somehow it seemed as if they couldn't have got through the day without that. Whatever their mood might be, the last glimpse of her face was sure to warm them like sunshine.

CHAPTER 4

The Laurence Boy

"WHAT in the world are you going to do now, Jo?" asked Meg one snowy afternoon, as her sister tramped through the hall in rubber boots, old coat and hood.

"Going out for exercise," answerd Jo, with a mischievous twinkle in her eyes and flourishing a broom in one hand, a shovel in the other.

With great energy Jo began to dig a path in the new-fallen snow all around the garden. Beyond the low green garden hedge, rising high on its hilly slope, was the stately stone mansion of the old gentleman, Mr. Laurence.

To Jo, this fine house seemed a kind of enchanted palace, full of splendours no one enjoyed. She had long wanted to behold the hidden glories and to know the Laurence boy. Since the Gardiner's party she was more eager than ever; but a week had gone by, and she had not caught a glimpse of him. As she dug her snowy way to the hedge, she made her plans. Mr. Laurence was out—she had seen him drive off. The servants were out of sight—no human was visible except the black-haired boy looking wistfully out of an upper-storey window.

Jo picked up a handful of soft snow and aimed it straight for the big house. The eyes at the window brightened, the lips widened in a smile.

"Are you sick?" Jo called out.

Laurie opened the window and croaked hoarsely, "Better, thank you. Bad cold. Been shut up all week."

"I'm sorry. What do you amuse yourself with? Do you read?"

"Not much. They won't let me."

"Can't somebody read to you?"

"Grandpa does sometimes—and Brooke. He's my tutor. Can't ask them all the time, though."

"Have some friends come and see you, then."

"Don't know anybody."

"You know us," began Jo.

"So I do! Will you come, please?" cried Laurie.

"I'll come if my mother will let me. I'll go ask her." And Jo shouldered her broom and marched into the house.

A few moments later she was ringing the Laurence doorbell and asking in a decided voice for "Mr. Laurie." A surprised servant came running up to Laurie's little parlour to announce a young lady.

"All right. Show her up. It's Miss Jo," said Laurie, and went to the door to meet Jo, who arrived with a covered dish in one hand and a basket containing Beth's three kittens in the other.

"Here I am, bag and baggage," she said briskly. "Mother sent her love. Meg wanted me to bring some of her blancmange, and Beth thought her cats would be comforting. I knew you'd laugh at them, but I couldn't refuse, she was so anxious to do something."

Beth's furry loan was just the thing, for in laughing over the kittens, Laurie forgot his bashfulness. When Jo uncovered the dish and showed him the creamy custard surrounded by a garland of green leaves and scarlet flowers from Amy's pet geranium, he said, "That looks too pretty to eat! Now, please take the big chair, and let me do something nice to amuse my company."

"No, I came to amuse you. Shall I read aloud?" Jo asked, eying a row of inviting books.

"If you don't mind, I'd rather talk."

"Not a bit," Jo answered gaily. "Beth says I never know when to stop talking."

"Is Beth the rosy one who stays home?"

"Yes, that's Beth—she's too bashful to go to school. She did her lessons at home with my father until he went away, then with my mother. Now Marmee is busy at the Soldiers' Aid Society, and Beth gets along alone as best she can. She is never idle or lonely for she has her dolls, her kittens, and her music. Her dolls are all outcasts, but she cherishes them more tenderly for that very reason. Beth's my girl, and a regular good one she is, too."

"The pretty one is Meg, and the curly-haired one is Amy, I believe?"

"How did you find that out?"

Laurie coloured up. "I often hear you calling to one another, and when I'm alone I can't help looking over at your house. When the lamps are lighted, before the curtains are drawn, it's like looking at a picture—to see the fire and all of you around the table with your mother. I can't help watching, though I beg your pardon for being so rude. I haven't any mother, you know."

The look in his eyes went straight to Jo's warm heart. "We'll never draw that curtain any more," she said. "I just wish, though, you'd come over and see us. Beth would sing to you if I begged her to, and Amy would show you her pictures. She loves to draw, and we call her our Raphael. Meg and I would make you laugh over our funny theatricals, and we'd have jolly times. Would your grandfather let you?"

"I think he would. He's just afraid I might be a bother to strangers—"

"But we aren't strangers. We're neighbours." Jo talked on and gave him a lively description of their household and of their great-aunt for whom she worked and the rude parrot and the library where she snatched precious hours for reading.

"If you like books so much, come down and see ours. Grandpa is out, so you needn't be afraid," said Laurie.

"I'm not afraid of anything," returned Jo, with a toss of her head.

"I don't believe you are!" the boy exclaimed admiringly and led the way down the stairs and through room after room of the house. When they came to the library, Jo clapped her hands with delight. The room was lined with books, and there were pictures and statues and a great open fireplace. Suddenly a bell rang, and Jo exclaimed with alarm, "Mercy me! It's your grandfather!"

"What if it is? You're not afraid of anything, you know," returned Laurie, looking wicked.

It was not Mr. Laurence, however, but the doctor who had come to see Laurie.

The boy excused himself, "Would you mind if I left you for a bit?"

"Not at all. I'm happy as a cricket here." She was standing before a fine portrait of old Mr. Laurence when the door opened again. Without turning, she said, "I'm sure now I wouldn't be afraid of him. He's got kind eyes though he looks as if he has a tremendous will of his own! He isn't as handsome as my grandfather. But I like him."

"Thank you, ma'am," said a gruff voice behind her and there, to her dismay, stood Mr. Laurence. Poor Jo blushed till she couldn't blush any redder.

"So you're not afraid of me, hey?"

"Not much, sir."

"And you don't think me as handsome as your grandfather?"

"Not quite, sir."

"And I have a tremendous will, have I? But you like me in spite of it?"

"Yes, I do, sir."

Her answers pleased the old gentleman. "You've got your grandfather's spirit, if you haven't his face," he said. "He was a brave man and an honest one, and I was proud to be his friend—What have you been doing to this boy of mine?" he asked in a sharper tone.

"Only trying to be neighbourly, sir! He seems a little lonely. We're only girls, but we would be glad to help if we could, for we haven't forgotten the splendid Christmas present you sent us," answered Jo eagerly.

"Tut, tut! That was the boy's affair. I shall come and see your mother sometime. Tell her so. There's the tea bell. Come down and go on being neighbourly."

"If you'd like to have me, sir."

"Wouldn't ask you, if I didn't," Mr. Laurence barked, and offered his arm. Laurie came running downstairs. He started in surprise at the sight of Jo on the arm of his grandfather, marching in triumph down to tea.

When they rose from the table, Jo proposed to go, but Laurie led her to the conservatory and cut an armful of roses and heliotrope. "Please give these to your mother and tell her I like the medicine she sent me very much."

They found Mr. Laurence in the drawing room standing before the fire. But Jo had eyes only for the grand piano. "Do you play?" she asked Laurie.

"Sometimes."

"Play for me now, so I can tell Beth."

So Laurie played—and remarkably well. Jo was extravagant in her praise until Mr. Laurence said, with an air of displeasure, "That will do, young lady. The boy's music isn't bad, but I hope he'll do well in more important things."

CHAPTER 5

Beth Finds the Palace Beautiful

WHEN all the afternoon's adventures had been told, the March family felt inclined to go visiting in a body, for each found something very attractive in the big house on the other side of the hedge. Mrs. March wanted to talk of her father with the man who had not forgotten him. Meg longed to walk in the conservatory among the flowers. Beth sighed for the grand piano, and Amy was eager to see the fine pictures and statues.

"Marmee," Jo asked with a troubled frown, "why did Mr. Laurence glower so, when I praised Laurie's music? He plays beautifully, but when I said so, it made the old gentleman quite short-tempered."

"I'm not sure, Jo, but I think it was because Laurie's father married an Italian musician, which displeased the old man. The lady was good and lovely and accomplished, but Mr. Laurence never saw his son after the marriage. Laurie's mother and father both died when he was a little child, and then his grandfather took him home. I dare say the old gentleman is afraid Laurie may want to be a musician, too."

"Let him if he wants to! And not plague his life out sending him to college when he hates to go," said Jo bluntly.

"That was a nice little speech the boy made about the medicine Mother sent him," said Meg, who at sixteen was a little sentimental.

"He meant the blanc-mange, I suppose," said Jo.

"I never saw such a girl, Jo! He meant you, of course. You don't know a compliment when you get one."

"I think they are great nonsense, and I'll thank you not to be silly and spoil my fun."

"It's like Pilgrim's Progress," murmured Beth who had not listened to a word that had been said. "We got out of the Slough of Despond and up the steep hill by trying to be good, and the house over there may be our Palace Beautiful!"

"We have to get by the lions first," laughed Jo, as if she enjoyed the prospect.

The big house did prove a Palace Beautiful, though it took some time for Beth

to pass the lions. Old Mr. Laurence was the biggest one. After he came to call and talked over old times with their mother, nobody felt much afraid of him except timid Beth. The new friendship with Laurie flourished like grass in spring.

What good times they had! Such plays and sleigh rides, such pleasant evenings in the old parlour and gay little parties at the great house. Meg could spend hours in the conservatory among the flowers. Amy copied pictures to her heart's content, and Jo browsed in the library.

But Beth could not get up courage to enter the Palace Beautiful. Everyone began to think she'd never get past "the fearsome lions" when somehow word of her timidity came to Mr. Laurence's ear. He set about mending matters. During one of the brief calls he made, he led the conversation to music and told such gay stories that Beth came out of her corner to listen.

She came closer and closer until she stood, wide-eyed, behind his chair. The artful old gentleman took no more notice

of her than if she'd been a fly. Presently, as if the idea had just occurred to him, he remarked to Mrs. March, "Laurie is neglecting his music now, and I'm glad of it. But the piano suffers for want of use. Wouldn't some of your girls like to run over and practise on it now and then, just to keep it in tune, ma'am?"

Beth took a step forward and pressed her hands together. The thought of practising on that splendid piano quite took her breath away.

"They needn't see or speak to anyone," the old gentleman went on. "Please tell the young ladies what I said. If they don't care to come, never mind."

With a nod and a smile, he rose to go, and Beth made up her mind to speak.

"Oh, sir, they do care, very, very much."

"Are you the musical girl?" he asked, as if he were just aware of her presence.

"I'm Beth. I love it dearly, and I'll come if you're quite sure nobody will hear me play."

"Not a soul, my dear."

"How kind you are." Beth slipped her little hand in his. She had no words to thank him.

The old gentleman softly stroked her hair and said in a tone few people ever heard, "I had a little girl once with eyes like these. God bless you, my dear. Good day, ma'am." And away he went in a great hurry.

Next day, after two or three retreats, Beth went in by the side door and at last touched the great instrument. Straightway she forgot her fears and after that first happy hour, the little brown hood slipped through the hedge nearly every day. She never knew that old Mr. Laurence often opened his study door to hear the sweet tunes, or that Laurie stood guard in the hall so that she wouldn't be disturbed, or that the new, easy pieces found themselves on the piano just for her.

"Marmee," Beth said one evening, "I'm going to work Mr. Laurence a pair of slippers. I don't know any other way of thanking him. Can I do it?"

The pattern was chosen—a cluster of pansies on a purple background—and Beth embroidered early and late until the slippers were finished. With Laurie's help they were smuggled onto the old man's study table with a short, simple note.

All day passed and the next before any acknowledgment came from the big house. On the afternoon of the second day, Beth went out on an errand. As she came up the street on her return, she saw four heads, popping in and out of the parlour windows.

"Here's a letter from Mr. Laurence! Come quick!" several voices cried.

"Oh, Beth, he's sent you—" Amy began, but she got no further, for Jo slammed shut the window.

At the door her sisters seized Beth and bore her to the parlour. The shy girl turned pale with delight, for there stood a little cabinet piano with a letter addressed to "Miss Elizabeth March " lying on its lid:

Miss March:
Dear Madam—

I have had many pairs of slippers in my life, but I never had any that suited so well as yours. Heart's-ease is my favourite flower, and these will always remind me of the gentle giver. I like to pay my debts, so I know you will allow me to send you something which once belonged to the little granddaughter I lost.

Your grateful friend and humble servant,

James Laurence.

CHAPTER 6

Amy's Catastrophe

IF anybody had asked Amy what the greatest trial of her life was, she would have answered at once, "My nose." No one minded it but herself, but Amy felt deeply the want of an aristocratic Grecian nose and drew whole sheets of handsome ones to console herself.

She had a decided talent for drawing. In the private school she attended, her teachers complained that instead of doing her sums, she covered her slate with animals. But she did her lessons fairly well and was popular with her schoolmates, who admired her little airs and graces, as well as the funny drawings that fell out of her books at unlucky moments.

One evening she looked up from her lessons with a deep sigh.

"What's wrong, dear?" Meg asked. She was Amy's special confidante, as Jo was gentle Beth's.

"I was just wishing that we were rich," Amy answered. "I need money so much. I'm dreadfully in debt."

"In debt, Amy?" Meg looked sober.

"I owe at least a dozen pickled limes, and I can't pay them without money."

Meg tried not to smile. "Are pickled limes the fashion now?"

Amy nodded. "Everyone is sucking them at their desks or trading them off for pencils or paper dolls at recess. If one girl likes another, she gives her a lime. If she's mad at her, she eats one before her face without offering even a suck. They treat by turns, and I've had ever so many but haven't returned them."

"How much will pay them off?" asked Meg, taking out her purse.

"A quarter would more than do it." Amy's face lit up as her sister gave her the coin.

Next day she could not resist the temptation of displaying the moist paper parcel as she hid it in her desk. The rumour went round that Amy March had twenty-four delicious limes and was going to treat.

The attentions of her friends—and even of her enemy, Jenny Snow—became overwhelming. But Amy crushed the Snow girl's hopes with a withering whisper, "You needn't be so polite all of a sudden, for you won't get any of my limes."

Now Mr. Davis, the teacher, just the week before had forbidden limes to be brought into the schoolroom. He had succeeded in banishing chewing gum, and

had waged a victorious war against the use of nicknames. Limes to him were worst of all, for he hated the odour of the fashionable pickle.

When Jenny Snow informed him in a loud whisper that Amy March had limes in her desk, his face flushed.

"Young ladies, attention, please." Fifty pairs of eyes were obediently fixed on his wrathful face.

"Miss March, bring the limes you have in your desk."

Despairingly Amy laid the bag of limes before him.

"Now take these disgusting things, two by two, and throw them out the window." Scarlet with shame and anger, Amy went to and fro twelve dreadful times and let the plump, juicy pickles fall from her reluctant hands. As she returned from her last trip, Mr. Davis rose and cleared his throat.

"Young ladies, you remember what I said to you a week ago. I am sorry this has happened, but I never break my word. Miss March, hold out your hand." Amy put both hands behind her. "Your hand, Miss March!"

Amy set her teeth, threw back her head, and bore without flinching several tingling blows on her palm. They were neither many nor heavy, but that made no difference. For the first time in her life, she had been struck.

"You will now stand on the platform till recess," he said.

During the minutes that followed, the proud and sensitive little girl suffered a terrible shame. The smart of her hand and the ache of her heart were forgotten in the dreadful thought: "I will have to tell at home and they will be so disappointed in me!" The fifteen minutes seemed an hour, but they came to an end at last.

"You can go, Miss March," said Mr. Davis, looking uncomfortable.

Amy went straight to the anteroom, snatched her things, and ran home, declaring she would never go to the school again.

The older girls held an indignation meeting at once. Mrs. March did not say much but looked disturbed, and comforted her unhappy daughter in her tenderest manner.

"It's perfectly maddening to think of all those lovely limes," sighed Amy, basking in the sympathy of her family.

"I am not sorry you lost them, for you broke the rules, and deserved some punishment," her mother replied.

"Do you mean you are glad I was disgraced before the whole school?" cried the young martyr.

"I don't approve of corporal punishment," said Mrs. March. "I dislike Mr. Davis' method of teaching, so I shall let you have a vacation from school. You may study at home with Beth. I shall ask your father's advice before I send you anywhere else."

The novelty of staying home was delightful for a few days, but studying with Beth or drawing could not occupy all of Amy's time, and she was often lonely. One Saturday afternoon she found Jo and Meg getting ready to go out with an air of secrecy that excited her curiosity. When she found out that Laurie had invited the older girls to go to the theatre to see *The Seven Castles*, she insisted upon going along.

"It's impossible, Amy, because you aren't invited. Next week you can go with Beth and Hannah—" Meg explained, but Jo snapped impatiently, "You can't go, so don't be a baby and whine."

"Please," Amy begged, "I'll be ever so good."

"I should think you'd hate to poke yourself where you aren't wanted," said Jo crossly. "Come on, Meg—there's Laurie now."

Her tone and manner angered Amy. As the two girls hurried down, she called over the banisters, "You'll be sorry for this, Jo March. See if you aren't."

"Fiddlesticks!" returned Jo, slamming the door.

On the way home, Jo wondered idly what Amy might have done to get even. Last time the younger girl had soothed her feelings by turning Jo's top bureau drawer upside down on the floor. But today, when they opened the front door, all seemed quiet, and Amy sat in the parlour reading. Jo decided that her little sister had forgiven and forgotten the quarrel.

There Jo was mistaken. Next day, when she went up to the garret to write a chapter in her book, the manuscript was not in its accustomed place. She raced downstairs and burst into the parlour. "Has anyone taken my book?" she demanded breathlessly.

Meg and Beth said "No" at once. Amy poked the fire and said nothing.

"Amy, you have it!" Jo said fiercely.

"No, I don't."

"You know where it is, then!" cried Jo, taking her by the shoulders and giving her a slight shake.

"You'll never see your silly book again," declared Amy. "I burnt it up."

"What! My book I worked over and meant to finish before Father got home?"

"I burnt it yesterday! I told you I'd make you pay for being so cross."

Amy got no further, for Jo's hot temper mastered her, and she shook the child till her teeth chattered, crying, "You wicked girl! I never can write it again, and I'll never forgive you as long as I live."

With a parting box on her sister's ear, Jo rushed out of the room up to the old sofa in the garret to sob out her grief and anger alone. Jo's book was her pride. It was only half a dozen tales but she had put her whole heart in the work, hoping to make something good enough to print. The loss was a real calamity, and Mrs. March soon brought Amy to a sense of the wrong she had done her sister.

When the tea bell rang and Jo appeared, Amy said meekly, "Please forgive me, Jo. I'm very, very sorry."

"I shall *never* forgive you," was Jo's stern answer.

33

All evening and all the next day she looked like a thundercloud and ignored Amy entirely. Everything went wrong for Jo that day. The morning was bitter cold, and she dropped her precious turnover. Aunt March was especially trying. Beth looked grieved when she got home.

"Everybody is so hateful, I'll ask Laurie to go skating," said Jo, and off she went.

Amy watched them leave with an exclamation of disappointment. "Jo promised I could go next time. But it's no use to ask such a crosspatch to take me," she mourned.

"It's hard for Jo to forgive the loss of her precious book," said Meg, "but I think she might be friends again if you try her at the right minute. Go after them and wait until Jo is feeling cheerful, skating with Laurie. Then ask her forgiveness again."

"I will," said Amy, and after a flurry to get ready, she ran after Jo and Laurie

who were just disappearing over the hill. Both had their skates on before Amy reached them, and Laurie was sounding the ice. Jo saw Amy coming and turned her back.

"I'll go on to the first bend to see if it's safe before we race," Laurie called.

Jo heard Amy fumbling with her skates, but she made no sign and zigzagged slowly down the river. Her anger had grown until it had taken possession of her.

As Laurie turned the bend, he shouted back, "Keep near the shore; it isn't safe in the middle."

Jo glanced over her shoulder. "No matter whether Amy has heard or not," her little demon of anger said, "let her take care of herself."

Jo was just at the bend when she saw Amy, far behind, skating out toward the smooth ice in the middle of the river! Thoroughly frightened, she turned back just in time to see Amy throw up her hands and go down with a sudden crash

34

of melting ice and a cry that made her sister's heart stand still. Laurie rushed past and called out, "Get a rail! Quick!"

How they did it, she never knew, but somehow they got Amy out of the freezing water, more frightened than hurt. Shivering, dripping, they walked the child home, and after an exciting time of it, she fell asleep, rolled in blankets.

During the bustle Jo had scarcely spoken. She had flown about looking pale and wild, her dress torn, her hands bruised. When Amy was comfortably asleep, the house quiet, and Mrs. March sitting by the bed, she called Jo to her to bind up the hurt hands.

"Are you sure she is safe?" whispered the unhappy girl.

"Quite safe."

"Laurie saved her," Jo sobbed. "If she had died, it would have been my fault. I let her go! It's my dreadful temper. I try to cure it, but then it breaks out worse than ever. Oh, Marmee, what shall I do?"

Mrs. March drew the dark head to her shoulder and kissed the wet cheek tenderly. "Jo dear, you think your temper is the worst in the world, but mine used to be just like it—"

"Yours? Why you are never angry!" Jo forgot her sorrow in surprise.

"I've learned not to show it. Your father helped me. I still hope not to *feel* angry, though it may take me another forty years!"

The patience and humility of the face she loved so well was a better lesson to Jo than the wisest lecture or the sharpest reproof.

"Oh, Mother, if I'm ever half as good as you, I shall be satisfied. I will try, but you must help me."

Amy stirred and sighed in her sleep, and Jo looked up with a troubled expression on her face. "I let the sun go down on my anger. I wouldn't forgive her, and today if it hadn't been for Laurie, it might have been too late!"

As if she had heard, Amy opened her eyes and held out her arms with a smile that went straight to Jo's heart. Neither said a word, but they hugged one another close, and everything was forgiven and forgotten in one hearty kiss.

CHAPTER 7

Meg Tries the Fashionable Life

"I DO think it was the most fortunate thing in the world for those King children to have the measles just now when Annie Moffat has invited me to the city," said Meg.

"A whole fortnight of fun will be splendid," replied Jo, as she folded skirts and laid them in Meg's trunk.

The girls had offered their choicest things to outfit their sister for the visit, and as they finished packing, they were filled with contentment.

"Let me see," said Meg. "There's the silk stockings and pretty carved fan and blue sash Mother gave me. And my new grey walking suit. Then my poplin for Sunday and for the small party. I did want the violet silk Marmee has been saving in the treasure chest, but there isn't time to make it over."

"Never mind," said Amy. "You've got your old tarlatan, and you look like an angel in white."

"It isn't low-necked, and it doesn't sweep enough, but it will have to do. My silk stockings and two pairs of new gloves are my comfort. You were a brick to lend me yours, Jo. There now," she said, as she laid snowy muslin nightcaps in the tray, "everything is ready."

The next day was fine, and Meg departed with Sallie Gardiner for her first taste of fashionable life in the city. The Moffats were *very* fashionable, and Meg was rather daunted at first by the splendour of the house. But they were kindly people and soon put their guest at ease.

The three young girls shopped, walked, rode and called on friends all day; went to theatres or operas in the evening.

Everyone petted Meg—or "Daisy," as they called her—and she was in a fair way to have her head turned. When the evening for the "small party" came, she found that the poplin wouldn't do at all. So out came the tarlatan, looking older and shabbier than ever beside Sallie's crisp new one. Meg saw the girls glance at it and then at one another, and her cheeks began to burn. The hard, bitter feeling of poverty was beginning when the maid brought in a box of flowers. Before she could speak, Annie had the cover off and was exclaiming at the lovely roses, heath, and fern within.

"For Belle, of course," she sighed, envying her older sister. "Her fiancé always sends her flowers, but these are the prettiest ever."

"They are for Miss March. And here's a note," said the maid, holding it out to Meg.

"What fun! Who are they from? Didn't know you had a beau!" cried the girls.

"The note is from my mother and the flowers from the Laurence boy," said Meg. Laurie had promised her flowers, and she was pleased that he remembered. Feeling almost happy again, she laid aside a few ferns and roses for herself and quickly made up bouquets for her friends. Somehow her dress no longer seemed old.

She danced to her heart's content that night and enjoyed herself until she overheard part of a conversation between Mrs. Moffat and Belle. "She coloured up quite prettily when the flowers came and pretended the note was from her mother," Belle was saying in an amused tone. "Poor thing—she would be nice looking if she was only got up in style. Do you think she'd be offended if we offered to lend her a dress for Thursday?"

"That dowdy tarlatan is all she has. She may tear it tonight, and that will be a good excuse for offering a decent one. Why not ask young Laurence? It would be amusing to watch them. I dare say the mother thinks he would be a good catch and has laid her plans," laughed Mrs. Moffat.

Meg's partner for the next dance appeared just then, so she heard no more. But she could not forget, and that night in bed she wept a few tears. Her resolution to be content with her simple wardrobe was weakened, her innocent friendship with Laurie seemed quite spoiled.

Next morning Belle said, "Mother has sent an invitation to your friend, Mr. Laurence, for Thursday."

Meg coloured but said teasingly, "She is very kind, but I'm afraid he won't come."

"Why not, Daisy dear?"

"He's too old—nearly seventy."

"You sly creature! Of course we meant the young man."

"There isn't any. Laurie is only a boy."

The girls exchanged glances. "About your age?"

"Nearer my sister Jo's. I will be seventeen in August."

"What shall you wear for Thursday?" Sallie asked, changing the subject.

"My white tarlatan again if I can mend it—it got sadly torn last night," said Meg, feeling very uncomfortable.

"Why don't you send home for another dress."

"I haven't any other." It cost Meg an effort to say that, but Belle broke in, "There's no need of sending home, Daisy, even if you had a dozen. I've a sweet blue silk I've outgrown, and you'll wear it to please me, won't you? I'd love to dress you up in style. With a touch here and there, you'd be a regular little beauty."

Meg couldn't refuse. She did long to see if she would be a "little beauty."

On Thursday evening, with the help of her French maid, Belle set out to turn Meg into a fine lady. They curled her hair, powdered her neck and arms, touched up her lips with coralline salve to make them redder. Then they laced her into Belle's low-necked, sky-blue dress, which was so tight she could hardly breathe. Bracelets, a necklace and earrings of silver, and a plumed fan followed.

"Come and show yourself," said Belle, leading the way and looking well pleased with her success.

In the drawing room, Meg felt as if she were acting in a play and enjoyed thoroughly her role of a fine lady. She was flirting her plumed fan and laughing at the jokes of her partner when suddenly, just opposite, she saw Laurie. Something in his honest eyes, as he looked at her in surprise and disapproval, made her blush. To complete her confusion, she saw Belle nudge Annie and remembered the conversation she had overheard.

"Silly creatures to put such thoughts in my head," Meg said to herself and rustled across the room to shake hands with her friend.

"I'm glad you came. I was afraid you wouldn't."

"Jo wanted me to come and tell her how you looked, so here I am," answered Laurie.

"What shall you tell her?" Meg asked.

"I shall say I didn't quite know you."

"Don't you like my dress?" asked Meg.

"No, I don't. I don't like fuss and feathers."

"You are the rudest boy I ever saw," Meg answered, and feeling very much ruffled, walked away.

She stood by the window, half hidden by the curtains, until Laurie came after her, saying with his very best bow, "Please forgive my rudeness and come dance with me."

"Take care my skirt doesn't trip you," Meg whispered. "I was a goose to wear it. Please don't tell them at home that I let the girls dress me up. I'd rather tell them myself and confess to Mother how silly I've been."

Though she danced and flirted and drank champagne with Ned Moffat and his friends, Meg didn't enjoy herself half as much as she had expected. On Saturday the visit was at an end, and Meg was glad to be home. When the younger girls had gone to bed, she told her mother and Jo everything.

Jo was indignant at what she called the silly rubbish, but Mrs. March looked grave. "I am more sorry than I can express for the mischief this visit may have done," she said.

"Don't be sorry," Meg answered. "I won't let it hurt me. I'll forget all the bad and remember only the good, for I did enjoy being praised and admired, and I can't help saying I liked that part."

"Mother," said Jo, "you don't have 'plans,' as that Mrs. Moffat said, do you?"

"Yes, Jo, all mothers do, but mine differ from Mrs. Moffat's, I suspect. I want my daughters to have a happy youth, to be well and wisely married, to lead useful lives with as little care and sorrow to try them as God sees fit to send. I *am* ambitious for you, but not to have you make a dash in the world. I'd rather see you poor men's wives if you were happy, than queens on thrones without self-respect and peace."

CHAPTER 8

The Post Office

SECRET societies were the fashion, and the March girls had thought it only proper to have one. As all of the girls admired Dickens' *Pickwick Papers*, which their father had read aloud over and over, they called themselves the Pickwick Club. They held their meetings in the garret on Saturday evenings, and these meetings were conducted with a good deal of ceremony. Three chairs were arranged in a row. A fourth chair, for the president, was at the table on which lay four white badges marked "P.C." and the weekly newspaper to which all contributed a poem or a story or notices of one kind or another.

At seven o'clock one Saturday evening in May, the four members marched up to the club room, solemnly tied on their badges, and took their seats. Meg, as the eldest, was Samuel Pickwick; Jo, being the literary member and editor of the newspaper, was Augustus Snodgrass; Beth, because she was round and rosy, was Tracy Tupman; and Amy, who was always trying to do what she couldn't, was Nathaniel Winkle.

The president, Mr. Pickwick, put on a pair of old spectacle frames and began to read the newspaper. Jo's long poem on page one contained an amusing verse about each member of the Pickwick Club.

A romantic tale signed "Samuel Pickwick" followed—the names of the hero and the fair lady being reminiscent of several of Shakespeare's better known plays. T. Tupman had contributed the history of a squash "eaten by a family named March," and Mr. Winkle had sent in a letter of apology in place of the story "he" meant to write. When the president finished reading the paper, Mr. Snodgrass rose.

"Mr. President and gentlemen," she said, "I wish to propose the admission of a new member—Mr. Theodore Laurence." As she heard a murmur of "No boys!" from the head table, Jo said with a sudden change of tone, "Come now, do have him—he wants most awfully to join."

"I'm afraid he'll laugh at our paper and make fun of us afterward," said Pickwick, pulling the little curl on her forehead, as she always did when doubtful.

Snodgrass replied earnestly, "Sir, I give you my word Laurie won't do anything of the sort. He does so much for us, I think the least we can do is to offer him a place here. Now then, let's vote. Remember it's our Laurie, and say 'Ay!'"

"Ay! Ay! Ay!" replied three voices at once.

"Good!" Snodgrass said and with a flourish threw open the door of the closet. There was Laurie sitting on the rag-bag, flushed and laughing.

"You rogue! You traitor! Jo, how could you!" cried the members of the club, as Jo led Laurie triumphantly to a chair and produced a badge for him.

The new member was equal to the occasion, however. Rising with a graceful bow to Mr. Pickwick, he said, "Mr. President and gentlemen, allow me to introduce myself as Sam Weller, your very humble servant. My friend and noble patron, Mr. Snodgrass, is not to be blamed for the base trickery practised here tonight. I planned it, but on my honour I will henceforth devote myself to the interest of this immortal club. As a slight token of my gratitude, I wish to say I have set up a post office in the lower corner of the garden. It's the old bird house, but I've fixed it up to hold letters, manuscripts, bundles—all sorts of things. Allow me to present the key to the club."

Great applause was in order as the new member took his seat, and no one ever regretted the admittance of Sam Weller.

The post office was a capital institution. Poetry and pickles, garden seeds and long letters, music, gingerbread and scoldings passed through the bird house. Old Mr. Laurence enjoyed the fun and amused himself by sending mysterious bundles. All spring, invitations were sent back and forth to picnics, tea parties, and boat rides on the river.

The first of June! This was a magic date in the March household. Meg's charges were off to the seashore, Aunt March set out in her carriage for Plumfield, her country house, and the older girls prepared for three months of vacation.

"What shall you do?" Amy asked, bringing in a pitcher of lemonade to celebrate the day.

"I shall lie abed late and do *nothing*," Meg answered.

"That wouldn't suit me," said Jo. "I've laid in a heap of books, and I'm going to spend hours reading in the old apple tree."

"May Beth and I play all the time and rest as the older girls mean to do?" Amy asked her mother.

"You may all try your experiment of all play and no work for a week," Mrs. March said, "and see how you like it!"

"It will be delicious," said Meg, and the rest agreed.

Next morning Meg stayed in bed until ten o'clock and had a solitary breakfast. But the room seemed lonely and untidy, for Jo had not brought in fresh flowers for the vases and Beth had not dusted.

Jo spent the morning on the river with Laurie and read in the apple tree all afternoon long.

Beth, rejoicing because she had no dishes to wash, gave herself a headache trying to learn four new songs at once. Amy put on her best dress, smoothed her curls, and went out to her honeysuckle bower to draw. She hoped someone would pass to admire her work, but her only visitor was a daddy longlegs who crawled across her paper.

That night they assured their mother that the experiment was working fine. However, as the week of idleness went on, the days kept growing longer and longer. No one would admit that she was tired of the experiment, but the truth was that by Friday night, the girls were glad the week was nearly done. Hoping to impress the lesson more deeply, Mrs. March tried an experiment of her own.

She gave Hannah a holiday, and next morning the girls found no fire in the kitchen, no breakfast in the dining room, and no mother anywhere to be seen.

Meg ran upstairs and came down again looking relieved but rather bewildered. "Mother isn't sick, only very tired. She says we must do the best we can for the day, taking care of ourselves."

"That's easy—I'm aching for something to do," admitted Jo—then added hurriedly, "Some new amusement, I mean."

There was food in the larder, and while Beth and Amy set the table, Meg and Jo prepared breakfast.

"First a tray for Marmee," said Meg. The tray looked pretty, but the tea was bitter and the omelette scorched.

"Poor little souls, they'll have a hard time of it, I'm afraid," Mrs. March said, when the young cook had hurried downstairs again to listen to complaints below.

"Never mind, I'll do the dinner," said Jo, who knew even less about cooking than Meg. "First I want to put an invitation in the post office for Laurie. We quarrelled yesterday, and a nice dinner will make up for it."

"You'd better see what you've got before you have company," said Meg.

"Oh, there's corned beef and plenty of potatoes, and I shall get some asparagus and a lobster for a salad. I'll have blancmange and strawberries for dessert." And Jo ran upstairs to ask her mother about ordering things.

"Get what you like and don't disturb me. I'm going out to dinner at Aunt Carrol's," said Mrs. March. "Hannah and I have had extra work to do all week. I'm going to take a vacation today and read, write, go visiting, and amuse myself."

Feeling strange and out of sorts, Jo hurried off to market and trudged home again with a very young lobster, some very old asparagus, and two boxes of strawberries.

The kitchen fire was out, the breakfast dishes piled up for washing. By the time she had rekindled the fire and cleared up the kitchen, it was time to begin dinner. Words cannot describe the anxieties and exertions Jo underwent. She boiled the asparagus for an hour. She hammered and poked the scarlet lobster shell and managed to get out a meagre portion that was almost buried in a forest of lettuce leaves.

She forgot the potatoes, and they had to be hurried so as not to keep the asparagus waiting. The blanc-mange was lumpy, and the strawberries not as ripe as they had looked in the market.

As dish after dish was tasted, poor Jo would have gladly gone under the table. Amy giggled, Meg looked distressed, loyal Beth struggled to choke down a few mouthfuls. Laurie talked and laughed, trying in vain to give a cheerful tone to the dinner.

Jo's strong point was the fruit, for she had sugared it well and there was a pitcher of thick cream to eat with it. Amy, who was fond of strawberries, took a heaping spoonful, choked and hid her face in her napkin.

"Oh, what is it?" exclaimed Jo, trembling with anxiety.

"Salt instead of sugar, and the cream is sour," replied Meg in a tragic voice.

Jo was on the verge of crying when the comical side of the affair suddenly struck her, and she laughed until the tears ran down her cheeks. So did everyone else, and the unfortunate dinner ended gaily with beef, bread and butter, and fun.

Mrs. March came home to find the girls hard at work cleaning up in the middle of the afternoon.

"Are you satisfied with your experiment, girls? Or do you want another week of idleness?" she said pleasantly, as Beth nestled up to her.

"I don't!" cried Jo.

"Nor I," echoed the others.

"You think then that it is better to have a few duties and live a little for others," said Mrs. March.

"Lounging and larking all day doesn't pay," Jo said decidedly. "I mean to go to work at something right off."

"Suppose you learn plain cooking," suggested Mrs. March, laughing gently, for Amy had poured out the dismal details of Jo's dinner party.

CHAPTER 9

Secrets

THE summer was a busy and happy one. Work mingled with play made the long days seem short. The garden post office was visited daily by Beth, who played postmistress. She liked the task of unlocking the little door and distributing the mail.

"Here's your posy, Marmee!" she said one midsummer morning. "Laurie never forgets. Miss Meg March, one letter and a glove," she continued, delivering the articles to her sister.

"Only one?" exclaimed Meg. "I left a pair in the conservatory. My letter is a translation of a German song I wanted. I think Mr. Brooke did it, for it isn't Laurie's writing."

"A letter for Jo, a book, and a funny old hat," said the postmistress, laughing.

"What a sly fellow Laurie is! I said I wished big hats were the fashion, and he has sent me this one." The letter was from her mother—a word of praise and encouragement that made the girl's heart glow. She *had* tried to control her temper and to be more ladylike, but she hadn't thought anyone had noticed. Reading in her little guidebook had helped, but this word from her mother made the burden seem light and the road easy.

The girls had not forgotten their play at being pilgrims. That very afternoon Laurie was swinging idly in a hammock when he saw the Marches come out of their house as if bound on an expedition. They carried long staffs, and each one had a linen bag slung over one shoulder. They walked quietly out the little back gate and began to climb the hill that lay between the house and the river.

"Well, that's cool!" said Laurie to himself. "To have a picnic and not ask me!"

Having nothing better to do, he roused himself to follow and see what the girls were up to. They were not at the river, and Laurie climbed the hill beyond to see if he could get a glimpse of them. A grove of pines covered one part of the hill, and here he caught sight of the four sisters, busily knitting or sewing.

Laurie advanced slowly. "May I come in, or shall I be a bother?"

"Of course," Jo said at once. "You can finish this story I'm reading aloud while I set the heel of my sock."

"It's against the rules to be idle here," Meg explained.

"Is it a game?" Laurie asked. "Do you come here often?"

"We bring our work here to be out of doors. For the fun of it, we bring our things in bags on our backs and carry staffs like pilgrims."

"I know," Laurie said. "Beth told me about your game of Pilgrim's Progress." He looked over the landscape. The wide blue river, the meadows on the other side, and the green hills beyond made a pretty picture. "How beautiful it all is," he said softly.

"We call this hill the 'Delectable Mountain,'" said Jo. "Christian's Celestial City is over there. Can you see the turreted castle waiting to receive the pilgrims? Wouldn't it be fun," she added, "if we could really live in the castles we make in the air?"

"I've made such quantities it would be hard to choose," Laurie said.

"You'd have to take your favourite. What is it?" spoke up Meg.

"If I tell mine, will you tell yours?"

"We will. You first, Laurie," said Jo.

Laurie considered a moment as he made himself comfortable on the soft carpet of pine needles. "My air castle is to live abroad and to have just as much music as I choose. What's yours, Meg?"

"I should like to have a lovely house full of luxurious things—pleasant people and heaps of money," she said.

"Wouldn't you have a master for your mansion in the air?" asked Laurie slyly, for he knew a secret and wondered if Meg guessed it.

"I said 'pleasant people.'" Meg leaned to tie her shoe so that no one saw her face.

"Why don't you say you'd have a splendid husband," Jo said bluntly. "That's what you mean."

"You'd have nothing but horses, inkstands, and reams of paper in your air castle," Meg retorted, a little sharply.

"Wouldn't I though! A stable full of Arabian steeds and a magic inkstand. I shall write books and get rich and famous. That's my favourite dream. I've got the key to my castle in the air," Jo added, "but whether I can unlock the door remains to be seen." She spoke mysteriously and would answer none of their questions, for, like Laurie, she too had a secret. If only she could make her dream come true!

Summer gave way to fall, and Jo was very busy in the garret. Seated on the old sofa one afternoon in October, she scribbled away until the last page of her manuscript was filled. She signed her name with a flourish and threw down her pen.

"There," she said to Scrabble, who was promenading the beams overhead, "I've done my best. If this won't suit, I shall have to wait till I can do better."

Lying back on the sofa, she read the pages carefully, making corrections here and there. Then she tied them up with a red ribbon and crept quietly downstairs.

She put on her hat and jacket noise-lessly and slipped out the side door. Taking a roundabout way to the road, she hailed a passing omnibus and rolled away to town. On alighting, she went at a great pace till she reached a certain number in a certain busy street. Having found the place, she stood in the doorway for a moment, then walked away as rapidly as she had come.

It happened that Laurie was looking out of the window of the building opposite, having come on some business for his grandfather. He watched Jo repeat her strange performance three times, then give herself a shake and resolutely mount the dirty stairs. A dentist's sign swung outside the building, and he decided that Jo had come to have a tooth out.

"It's like her to come alone," he said and went down to wait in the doorway. If she had a bad time of it, she'd welcome someone to see her home.

In a remarkably short time Jo reappeared, looking like a person who had just passed through a trying time. Laurie caught up with her.

"Was it very bad?" he asked with an air of sympathy.

"Not very."

"You got through quickly."

"Yes, thank goodness."

"Why did you come alone?" Laurie asked, as he fell into step beside her.

"Didn't want anyone to know."

"How many did you have out?"

Jo caught on to Laurie's mistake and laughed. "There are two which I want to come out. I must wait a week."

"What are you laughing at?" Laurie looked puzzled. "I don't believe you've been to the dentist at all. You are up to something. You can't hide anything, so confess, and I'll tell you a secret of my own."

"Is your secret a nice one?" Jo asked, tempted.

Laurie nodded. "All about people you know—I've been aching to tell it a long time. Come on, you begin!"

"You'll not say anything at home?" Jo took a deep breath. "I've left two stories with the editor of the *Spread Eagle*, and he's to give an answer next week!"

"Hurrah for the celebrated American authoress!" cried Laurie, throwing up his hat and catching it again.

"Hush," said Jo. "It won't come to anything, I dare say."

"It will! And won't we all feel proud to see your name in print!"

Jo's eyes sparkled at the words of encouragement. "Now tell your secret, Laurie. Play fair, or I'll never believe you again."

"I may get into a scrape for telling," Laurie said, "but I know where Meg's other glove is."

For the next fortnight she behaved so queerly that her sisters were quite bewildered. She rushed to the door when the postman rang and was rude to John Brooke whenever they met. Laurie and she were always flapping their wings and making mysterious signs to one another till Meg declared they had both lost their wits.

On the second Saturday the older sister was scandalized by the sight of Laurie chasing Jo all over the garden with a newspaper. In a few minutes Jo bounced in, dropped herself on the sofa, unfolded the newspaper, and began to read.

"What have you got?" Meg asked. "Is there anything interesting?"

"Only a story," Jo mumbled, keeping the name out of sight.

"What's it called?" asked Beth.

" 'The Rival Painters,' " said Jo.

"Is that all?" Jo was disappointed.

"It's quite enough for the present—Brooke carries it in the pocket over his heart! He's had it all summer. Isn't that romantic?"

"No," Jo said fiercely. "It's horrid. It's ridiculous. It won't be allowed. I wish you hadn't told me."

"I thought you'd be pleased."

"At the idea of anybody coming to take Meg away? No, thank you. I don't think secrets agree with me," Jo said unhappily.

"That sounds good," Meg said. "Read it out loud."

Jo began to read very fast. The girls listened with interest, for the tale was romantic and somewhat pathetic.

Meg wiped a tear away as the lovers met their sad end. "Viola and Angelo are two of *our* favourite names," she said. "Isn't that queer?"

"Who wrote it?" asked Beth suddenly, as she caught a glimpse of Jo's face.

Jo sat up very straight and answered in a loud voice, "Your sister."

"I knew it! I knew it!" cried Beth. "Oh my Jo, I am so proud!"

Meg couldn't believe it until she saw the words "Miss Josephine March" actually printed in the paper.

How delighted they all were as the paper passed from hand to hand! How proud Mrs. March was when she saw it!

Having told how she took the tales to the newspaper editor, Jo added, "The man wrote me that he liked them both but didn't pay beginners. So I let him print the two stories anyway and today this paper came and Laurie caught me with it and insisted on seeing it. And I shall write more—and he's going to get the next paid for. And I'm so happy, for in time I may be able to support myself and help the girls, and—"

Her breath quite gave out, and she hid her head in the sofa pillow so that the others could not see the tears of happiness in her eyes.

CHAPTER 10

The Telegram

ONE dreary November day, Laurie appeared at the March house to invite the girls for a drive.

"I'm going to take Brooke home," he said. "Meg, you'll go, won't you?"

Meg whisked out her workbasket. "Thank you, but I'm busy," she said hurriedly. Laurie's tutor made her feel shy and young.

"Come on, the rest of you," Laurie urged.

"Of course we'll come," said Jo, and the three went off to get ready.

Laurie leaned over Mrs. March's chair affectionately. "Is there anything we can do for you on the way, ma'am?"

"No, thank you," Mrs. March answered. "Except call at the post office, if you'll be so kind. It's our day for a letter from my husband, and the postman passed us by."

A sharp ring at the door interrupted her, and a minute later Hannah came in.

"It's one of them horrid telegraph things," she said, holding the envelope as if she were afraid it might explode.

At the word "telegraph," Mrs. March ripped it open, read the two lines and dropped back, white and trembling.

Jo took the message as it fell from her mother's hand and read aloud in a frightened voice:

Mrs. March:
Your husband is very ill. Come at once.
        S. Hale
        Blank Hospital, Washington

How still the room was as they listened; how strangely the day darkened outside! How suddenly the whole world seemed to change! Mrs. March stretched out her arms to her daughters. "I shall go at once," she said, "but it may be too late. Oh, children, children, help me to bear it."

Words of comfort died away in tears. Hannah was the first to recover. "The Lord keep the dear man! I won't waste no time, but will get your things ready right away, ma'am."

"Hannah's right. There's no time for tears now. Be calm, girls," Mrs. March said bravely, "and let me think. . . . Where's Laurie?" she asked, after a moment's silence.

"Here, ma'am. What can I do?"

"Send a telegram saying I will come at once. The next train leaves early in the morning. I'll take that."

"What else?" the boy asked, looking ready to fly to the ends of the earth.

"Leave a note at Aunt March's," Mrs. March said, as Jo held out her notebook and a pen. Mrs. March wrote a few lines and gave the paper to Laurie.

"Now go, dear, and don't drive too fast. There is no need for a desperate pace. Jo, run to the Aid Society and tell Mrs. King I can't come. On the way, get the things I've written down. I must go prepared for nursing, for hospital stores are not always good. Beth, go ask Mr. Laurence for a couple of bottles of good wine. I'm not too proud to beg for Father. Amy, tell Hannah to get down the trunk, and Meg, come help me pack."

They scattered like leaves before a gust of wind, and the quiet, happy household was broken as if the telegram had cast an evil spell.

Mr. Laurence came hurrying back with Beth, bringing every comfort he could think of. There was nothing he didn't offer, from his own dressing gown to himself as escort.

At the thought of having an escort, Mrs. March's eyes brightened with relief. But she shook her head. "I cannot hear of you undertaking the long journey," she said firmly.

Mr. Laurence knit his brows, then marched abruptly out of the house. "Be back directly," he muttered.

No one had time to think of him again until Meg, coming through the hall with a pair of rubbers in one hand and a cup of tea in the other, came suddenly upon John Brooke.

"I came to offer myself as escort to your mother, Miss March. Mr. Laurence has commissions for me in Washington, and it will give me real satisfaction to be of service to her there."

Down dropped the rubbers, and the tea was very near to following, as Meg put out her hands with a face so full of gratitude that Mr. Brooke blushed with pleasure and embarrassment.

Everything was arranged by the time Laurie returned with a note from Aunt March enclosing the sum of money needed for the journey, but repeating what she had said so many times before—that it was absurd for her nephew to have gone into the Army, she had always predicted that no good would come of it, and she hoped they'd take her advice next time.

The note went into the fire, the money in her purse, and Mrs. March went on with her preparations with tightly folded lips.

"Oh, Jo, how could you? Your one beauty," whispered Meg.

"My dear girl," Mrs. March said with trembling lips, "there was no need of this."

Beth hugged the cropped head tenderly. "She doesn't look like my Jo, but I love her dearly for it."

Jo's indifferent air deceived no one. She rumpled up the short brown mop. "It doesn't affect the fate of the nation," she murmured stoutly. "I was getting too proud of my long hair. The barber said I could soon have a curly crop which will be boyish and easy to keep in order. I'm satisfied, so please take the money, and let's have supper."

"What made you do it?" asked Amy, who would as soon have thought of cutting off her head as her pretty yellow curls.

Dusk fell on the house, and still Jo did not come. Laurie went off to find her, for no one knew what strange notion Jo might take into her head.

He missed her, however, and she came walking in with a very queer expression. Without removing her bonnet or cloak, she laid a roll of bills before her mother, saying with a little choke in her voice, "That's my contribution toward making Father comfortable and bringing him home."

"My dear, where did you get it? Twenty-five dollars! Jo, I hope you haven't done anything rash?"

"No. I didn't beg, borrow, or steal it. I don't think you'll blame me, for I only sold what was my own."

As she spoke, Jo took off her bonnet. All of her long, thick chestnut hair was cut off.

"Your hair! Your beautiful hair!" Amy wailed.

"Well, I was wild to do something for Father," replied Jo. "I hated your having to borrow from Aunt March, for she always croaks. I was bound to have some money, even if I sold the nose off my face. I hadn't the slightest idea of selling my hair, but in a barber's window I saw tails of hair not so thick as mine for forty dollars. I walked in and asked if they bought hair and what they'd give for mine. The barber didn't want to buy at first. I begged him to and told him why I was in such a hurry. His wife heard me and said, 'Take it, Thomas, and oblige the young lady.' Their son is in the Army, and she talked away about him all the time the man clipped."

"Didn't you feel dreadful when the cutting began?" Meg asked in a sympathetic voice.

"I'll confess I felt queer when I saw my hair laid out on the table," Jo answered. "The woman gave me a lock to keep. I'll give it to you, Marmee."

Mrs. March folded the wavy chestnut lock and laid it away in her desk. Something in her face made the girls change the subject and talk about Mr. Brooke's kindness in going as escort and the happy times they'd have when their father could be brought home.

When they were in bed for a few hours' sleep before Mrs. March's departure, Jo lay motionless, and Meg thought she was asleep until a stifled sob broke the stillness.

Meg reached out and touched the wet cheek. "Jo, dear, what is it? Are you crying about Father?"

"No, not now."

"What, then?"

"My—my hair!" burst out poor Jo. "I'm not sorry. I'd do it again tomorrow if I could. It's only the vain part of me that goes and cries in this silly way."

In the cold grey dawn, the lamps in the March household were lit. The big trunk was ready in the hall. Hannah flew about the kitchen with her nightcap on, making tea.

Nobody talked much, but as Mr. Laurence's carriage drew up at the door and Mr. Brooke leaped out, Mrs. March said, "Children, I leave you to Hannah's care and Mr. Laurence's protection. Don't grieve and fret while I am gone. Meg dear, watch over your sisters. Be patient, Jo, write me often, and be my brave girl, ready to help and cheer us all. Beth, comfort yourself with your music, and you, Amy, be obedient and keep happy and safe at home."

Laurie and his grandfather came in to see the travellers off, and Mr. Brooke looked so strong and sensible that the girls christened him "Mr. Greatheart" on the spot.

"Good-bye, my darlings!" whispered Mrs. March. "God bless and keep us all!"

CHAPTER 11

Dark Days

"I FEEL as if there had been an earthquake," said Jo, as the carriage rolled away and was lost to sight in the early morning fog. "It seems as if half the house was gone."

Beth opened her lips to say something, but could only point to the pile of nicely mended stockings which lay on their mother's table, showing that even in her last hurried moments she had thought of them. It was a little thing, but it went straight to their hearts. In spite of brave resolutions, they broke down and cried.

Hannah came to the rescue, armed with a coffee pot. "Now, my dear young ladies, remember what your ma said, and don't

fret. Have a cup of coffee all around, and then let's fall to work." Coffee was a treat, and they all drew up to the table.

"'Hope and keep busy'; that's the motto for us," said Jo. "I shall go to Aunt March's as usual. Won't she lecture!"

"I shall go to the Kings," Meg said, "though I'd much rather stay home and attend to things."

"No need of that," Amy put in with an important air. "Beth and I can keep house perfectly well—with Hannah to tell us what to do."

The two older girls set out with their turnovers. They looked sorrowfully back at the window, expecting it to be empty.

But there was Beth, waving as their mother was accustomed to do.

"That's so like my Beth!" said Jo, waving her hat and letting her close-cropped hair blow in the wind.

News from Washington came, comforting news. Though dangerously ill, their father had already improved under Mrs. March's tender care. Mr. Brooke wrote every day, and as head of the family, Meg insisted on reading the messages aloud. Jo watched her sister jealously, and it seemed to her that Meg valued the letters because John Brooke wrote them quite as much as for their cheering words.

For the first week, each of the girls wrote long letters. They read in their little guidebooks, attended to their duties and, indeed, were models of virtue. Little by little, however, they began to fall back into the old ways. Only Beth seemed to take on her mother's outside duties as well as her share of the housekeeping.

One cold afternoon, when the older girls were comfortably toasting their toes by the fire, Beth quietly slipped out with a basket of food for the Hummel children. She had been going every day, for the baby was sick and Mrs. Hummel went out to work, leaving the other children to care for it. Beth had suggested that Jo or Meg go along, but they had put it off for another time.

It was late when she came back, and no one saw her go upstairs and shut herself in her mother's room. Half an hour later, Jo found her sitting near the medicine chest in her mother's closet. Her eyes were red from weeping, and she had a medicine bottle in her hand.

"Christopher Columbus! What's the matter?" Jo cried.

"You've had scarlet fever, haven't you?" Beth asked in a small voice.

"Years ago, when Meg did. Why?"

"Oh, Jo, the baby's dead!" Beth sobbed.

"What baby?"

"Mrs. Hummel's; it died in my lap before she got home."

Jo took her sister in her arms and said remorsefully, "My poor dear! How dreadful for you. I ought to have gone."

"It wasn't dreadful, Jo, just so sad. The little thing seemed asleep, but all of a sudden it gave a little cry and then lay very still. We tried to give it some milk, but it didn't stir. I knew it was dead. Then Mrs. Hummel came with the doctor."

"Don't cry, Beth."

"The doctor said the baby had had scarlet fever and scolded Mrs. Hummel for not calling him before. She told him she was too poor to pay, and then he was kinder and looked at the other children's throats. Then he turned suddenly on me and told me to go right home and take belladonna or I'd have the fever."

"No, you won't," cried Jo, hugging her close with a frightened look. "Oh, Beth, I'll never forgive myself if you get sick! If Mother was only at home!"

Jo went to consult Hannah and Meg. "Now I'll tell you what we'll do," said Hannah calmly. "We'll have Dr. Bangs just to take a look at Beth. And we'll send Amy off to your Aunt March's for a spell to keep her out of harm's way. One of you girls can stay home and amuse Beth for a day or two. We'll keep her in bed."

"I'll stay, I'm oldest," said Meg.

"No, I shall," Jo interrupted. "It's all my fault if she's sick. I told Marmee I'd take care of things—instead I stayed home and amused myself writing rubbish."

Beth did have the fever and was much sicker than anyone but Hannah and Dr. Bangs suspected. Very little was known about scarlet fever. Dr. Bangs did his best, but left a good deal to Hannah's experienced nursing.

Hannah wouldn't hear of Mrs. March's being told. "Your father needs her, girls," she said, "and we can take care of Beth." So Meg and Jo wrote daily letters to Washington without any mention of the illness. They did not think it right to deceive their mother but had been bidden to obey.

Jo devoted herself to Beth day and

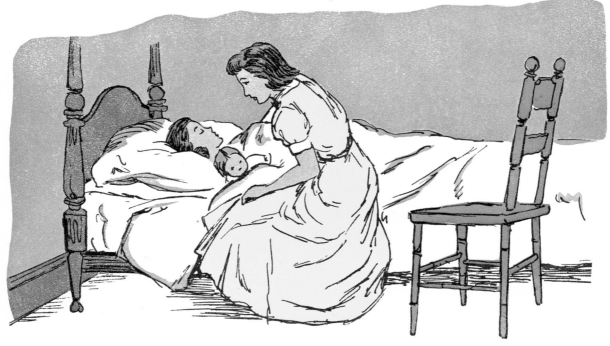

how she did. Poor Mrs. Hummel came daily to inquire, and the neighbours sent all sorts of comforts.

Dr. Bangs came twice a day, Hannah sat up at night, Meg kept a telegram ready to send her mother, but Hannah still said, "There's not any danger yet."

The first of December was a wintry, stormy day. Beth tossed to and fro in a heavy sleep. Jo, who never left her side, bent to hear the meaningless words on her parched lips.

When Dr. Bangs came that morning, he held Beth's hot hand in his a moment and laid it gently down, saying in a low tone to Hannah, "If Mrs. March *can* leave her husband, she'd better be sent for."

Meg dropped into a chair at the sound of those words. Hannah nodded without speaking. But Jo ran to the parlour,

night—not a hard task, for the little girl was very patient. But there came a time when she did not know the familiar faces and began to play on the coverlet as if on her beloved piano, and begged hoarsely for her mother. Jo grew frightened. Meg wanted to write the truth. Still, Hannah said she wouldn't think of troubling Mrs. March.

A letter from Washington added to their anxiety, for their father was worse. How dark the days seemed, how heavy the hearts of the sisters as they worked and waited! And Amy in her exile longed to be home, remembering with grief how many neglected tasks Beth's willing hands had done for her.

Laurie haunted the house; Mr. Laurence locked the grand piano until Beth could play it again. Everyone missed the rosy-cheeked little girl. The milkman, the grocer, the butcher and baker inquired

snatched up the telegram, and rushed out into the storm to send the message.

She was just returning to the house when Laurie came in, bringing a letter which said that Mr. March was mending again. Jo looked up from reading it with a face so full of misery that Laurie asked quickly, "What is it? Is Beth worse?"

"I've sent for Mother."

"Good for you, Jo!"

"The doctor told us to."

"Oh, Jo, is it as bad as that?" Laurie looked startled.

As the tears streamed down poor Jo's cheeks, she stretched out her hand in a helpless sort of way. Laurie took it in his, saying, "I'm here. Hold on to me, Jo."

"I can't let Beth go, I can't, I can't," sobbed Jo.

"Beth is not going to die. I'm sure she's not," Laurie whispered. "And tonight, I'll give you something that will warm the cockles of your heart." Laurie spoke in such a strange tone that Jo looked up through her tears.

"What is it?" she cried.

"I telegraphed your mother yesterday, and Brooke answered that she'd come at once, and she'll be here tonight, and everything will be all right. Aren't you glad I did it?"

"Oh, Laurie, I am so glad," Jo cried, and threw her arms around his neck. "You were such a dear to do it."

"I got fidgety," Laurie said, "and so did Grandpa. When he said it was high time something was done, I pelted over to the telegraph office. The late train comes in at two in the morning. I shall go for your mother."

"Laurie, you're an angel! How shall I ever thank you?"

CHAPTER 12

Mrs. March Returns

WITH Laurie's news, a breath of fresh air seemed to blow through the house and something better than sunshine brightened it. Jo set the sickroom in order. Meg stopped every now and again to re-read the message from Washington. Beth's bird began to chirp, and a half-open rose was discovered on Amy's bush in the window.

Every time the girls met, their pale faces broke into smiles as they hugged one another, whispering, "Marmee's coming! Marmee's coming!" And when Laurie went to tell Amy of her mother's expected arrival, the little exile cried for joy.

Everyone rejoiced but Beth. She lay in a heavy sleep, only rousing to mutter "Water!" with lips so parched they could hardly shape the word. Jo and Meg hovered over her as the snow fell; the bitter wind raged, and the hours dragged on.

At dusk, the doctor came in and said that some change, for better or worse, would probably take place about midnight, at which time he would return.

67

Every time the clock struck, Jo and Meg looked at each other with brightening eyes, for each hour brought help nearer. Hannah, quite worn out, lay on the sofa in Beth's room. Old Mr. Laurence marched to and fro in the parlour. Laurie lay on the rug, waiting for the time to meet the train.

"I wish I had no heart, it aches so," whispered Meg, by the bedside. "If God spares Beth, I never will complain again."

"If God spares Beth, I'll try to love and serve Him all my life," Jo answered solemnly. "But if life is often as hard as this, I don't see how we shall ever get through it."

The clock struck twelve. The house was as still as death. The front door closed softly as Laurie departed for the station. Another hour passed. Hannah slept on, and the two sisters watched Beth's face. It seemed to them that a slight change had come over her features, but they could not be sure.

It was past two when a great change seemed to take place. The fever flush and the look of pain were gone, and the beloved little face looked pale and peaceful. Was this death?

Hannah started out of her sleep and came over to look at Beth, feel her hands, listen at her lips. Then throwing her apron over her head, she exclaimed, "The fever's turned; she's sleeping natural; her skin's damp, and she breathes easy! Praise be given! Oh, my goodness me!"

At this moment, Dr. Bangs came to confirm the happy truth. The doctor was a homely man, but Jo thought his face quite heavenly when he smiled and said, "Yes, my dears, I think the little girl will pull through. Keep the house quiet, let her sleep. When she wakes give her—"

What they were to give, neither heard. They held each other close with hearts too full for words. When they looked at Beth again, she was lying as she used to do, with her cheek pillowed on her hand, breathing quietly, as if she had just fallen asleep.

"If Marmee would only come now!" said Jo.

Never had the sun risen so beautifully and never had the world seemed so lovely as it did to Meg and Jo as they looked out in the early morning. Meg brought Amy's rose that had blossomed in the night and put it in the vase by Beth's bed.

"When she wakes, the first thing she will see will be the little rose and Mother's face," she said softly.

"Listen!" cried Jo, starting to her feet. There was a sound of bells at the door below, a glad cry from Hannah and then Laurie's voice: "Girls, she's come! She's come!"

CHAPTER 13

Something in the Air

MEG's wish was realized, for when Beth woke, the first objects on which her eyes fell were the little rose and her mother's face. Too weak to wonder at anything, she only smiled and slept again. The girls waited upon their mother, for she would not unclasp the thin hand which clung to hers even in sleep.

As they fed Mrs. March the fine breakfast Hannah had dished up, they listened to her account of their father, of Mr. Brooke's promise to stay and nurse him, of

the comfort Laurie's hopeful face had given her when the train arrived, so long delayed by the storm.

At last with a blissful sense of burden lifted from them, Meg and Jo went off to sleep. Mrs. March left her chair by Beth's bedside in the late afternoon to visit Amy. The little exile had been having a difficult time of it under Aunt March's stern discipline and testy temper, but it was all forgotten at the sight of her mother. She had tried to be patient and obedient, and in this she had succeeded. After all the news about Beth and her father had been told, Amy showed her mother a ring of sky-blue turquoise stones, with a quaint golden guard, on her plump little finger.

"Aunt March gave it to me today," Amy said. "She called me to her and kissed me and said I was a credit to her. I'd like to wear it, Marmee. May I?"

"It is very pretty," her mother answered thoughtfully, "but I think you are rather young for such ornaments."

"I'll try not to be vain," said Amy. "I want to wear it to remind me of something."

"Aunt March?" asked her mother, laughing.

"No, to remind me not to be selfish. Beth isn't selfish, and that's the reason everyone loves her. I'm going to try to be like Beth, and if I had something always to remind me, I think I could do better."

"Wear your ring, then, dear. The wish to be good is half the battle. Now, I must go back to Beth. Keep up your spirits, little daughter, and soon we'll all be together again."

That evening while Meg was writing to her father, Jo slipped upstairs into Beth's room. She stood a minute by her mother's chair, twisting her fingers in her short curls with a worried gesture.

"What is it, Jo?" Mrs. March asked.

"I want to tell you something, Mother."

"About Meg?"

"How quickly you guessed!"

"Ned Moffat hasn't been here, I hope?" Mrs. March spoke rather sharply. Ever since Meg's visit to the Moffats, Annie's older brother had shown an interest in Meg. Mrs. March had no wish to have Meg drawn into fashionable society.

"No," Jo answered. "If Ned had come, I would have shut the door in his face. It's something different. Last summer Meg left a pair of gloves next door and only one was returned. Laurie told me that Mr. Brooke had it. When Laurie teased him about it, Mr. Brooke confessed that he cared for Meg but didn't dare say so because she was young and he was so poor Isn't that a dreadful state of things?"

"Do you think Meg is interested in John?" Mrs. March asked calmly.

"*Who?*"

"Mr. Brooke. I call him John now. We fell into the way of doing so at the hospital, and he likes it."

"Oh, dear!" Jo cried. "I know you'll take his part. He's been good to Father, and you won't send him away but let him marry Meg if he wants to." Jo gave her hair a wrathful tweak.

"She'll see *his* feeling in those handsome brown eyes she talks about, and then it will be all up with her," Jo said gloomily. "Brooke will carry her off and make a hole in the family. Everything will be horribly uncomfortable." Jo shook her fist at the absent John.

"Your father and I have agreed that Meg shall not be married before she is twenty. If she and John love one another, they can wait and test their love." Mrs. March sighed. "I hope things go happily with her. I am content to see Meg begin humbly, for if I am not mistaken, she will be rich in the possession of a good man's heart, and that is better than a fortune."

Jo gave her mother a hug. "I wish wearing flat-irons on our heads would keep us from growing up. But buds will be roses and kittens, cats—more's the pity."

"My dear, don't get angry about it. John went with me at Mr. Laurence's request. He was so devoted to your father that we couldn't help getting fond of him. He told us that he loved Meg but would earn a comfortable home before he asked her to marry him. And before that, as soon as Laurie is ready for college, John is going off to the war. He only wanted our permission to love her and work for the right to make her love him if she could."

"I don't know anything about love and such nonsense," Jo muttered. "In novels girls blush, faint away, and act like fools. Meg does nothing of the sort. She eats and drinks and sleeps like a sensible creature and only blushes a little when Laurie teases her about 'that man.' I felt mischief was brewing, but it's worse than I had guessed."

Mrs. March smiled and smoothed her daughter's hair. "I prefer not to say anything to Meg yet. When John comes back and I see them together, I'll be able to judge better her feeling toward him."

CHAPTER 14

A Christmas Present for the March Family

LIKE sunshine after storm were the peaceful weeks that followed. Mr. March began to write of returning early in the new year. Beth improved rapidly and was soon able to lie on the study sofa all day, amusing herself with the cats and her family of bedraggled dolls. Meg cooked Beth's favourite dishes, while Amy celebrated her return by giving away as many of her treasures as her sisters would accept.

The memory of the conversation about Meg and John Brooke weighed on Jo's spirits. She kept silent, but she watched Meg for "symptoms." "I caught her singing that song he gave her, and once she said 'John' as you do," Jo reported gloomily to her mother. "She turned as red as a poppy! And the other day, when I was looking in her desk for stamps, I found a bit of paper scribbled over with the words 'Mrs. John Brooke.' Whatever shall we do?"

"Nothing but wait," her mother answered. "Father's coming will settle everything. Let's think now about Christmas and make it an especially happy one."

Several days of unusually fine weather ushered in a splendid Christmas Day. Beth, wrapped in her mother's gift—a soft, cherry-red dressing gown—was carried in triumph to the window to behold the offering of Jo and Laurie. They had made a stately snow maiden in the garden. Crowned with holly, she bore a basket of fruit in one hand and a great roll of new music in the other. A bright, woolly afghan was wrapped about her shoulders, and a pink paper streamer held this Christmas carol:

God bless you, dear Queen Bess!
May nothing you dismay,
But health and peace and happiness
Be yours, this Christmas Day.

Laurie ran in and out to bring in the gifts, and Jo recited silly speeches as she presented each one.

"I'm so full of happiness," said Beth, "that if Father were only here, I couldn't hold a drop more."

Half an hour later Laurie opened the parlour door and popped his head in. He said very quietly. "Here's another Christmas present for the March family." He might just as well have given an Indian war whoop, for his face and voice gave him away.

Before the words were out of his mouth, a tall man took his place, leaning heavily on the arm of another tall man, who tried to say something and couldn't. There was a general stampede as Mr. March became invisible in the embrace of loving arms. And for the next few minutes, everybody seemed to lose his wits. Jo nearly fainted and had to be comforted on Laurie's shoulder. Mr. Brooke kissed Meg entirely by mistake. Amy tumbled over a stool and never stopping to get up, hugged her father's boots contentedly.

Suddenly Mrs. March remembered Beth, who had been carried to the next room to rest on the sofa. But joy had put strength into the feeble limbs. The little red wrapper appeared on the threshold, and Beth ran straight into her father's arms.

There never was such a Christmas dinner as they had that day. Mr. Laurence and Laurie dined with them, and also Mr. Brooke—at whom Jo glowered darkly. As twilight gathered, the guests departed, and the happy family sat together around the fire.

"This year has been rather a rough road for you to have travelled, my little pilgrims," Mr. March said. "But you have got on bravely."

"How did you know? Did Mother tell you?" asked Jo.

"A little, and I've made several discoveries today." Mr. March took Meg's hand. "Here's one," he said. "I remember when your first care was to keep your hands white and smooth. They were pretty then, but to me much prettier now, for I read usefulness in these hands."

"What about Jo? Please say something nice," whispered Beth in her father's ear.

"In spite of the curly crop, I don't see the tomboy I left a year ago," said Mr. March. "I rather miss my wild girl, but I have a strong, helpful, tender-hearted woman in her place."

Jo's thin face grew rosy in the firelight as she received her father's praise.

"Now Beth," said Amy, longing for her own turn.

Mr. March just held the little girl close. "I've got you safe, my Beth, and I'll keep you so, please God."

After a minute's silence he looked down at Amy. "I observed that Amy took drumsticks at dinner, though she prefers the breast. I also observe that she does not think so often of her looks, so I conclude that she has learned to think more of other people and less of herself."

"Do you remember," Beth said after a moment, "how after many troubles, Christian and Hopeful came to a pleasant green meadow where they rested before they went on to their journey's end? This is our Pleasant Meadow, isn't it?"

She slipped from her father's arms and went slowly to her little piano and, for the first time in many weeks, touched the keys. As they had always done in times past, the reunited family closed the day with a song.

CHAPTER 15

The Future Begins

ON the day after Christmas, the whole household had trouble settling down. The girls hovered about their father like bees over clover. Hannah kept popping her head in the study door "to peek at the dear man." Mrs. March beamed as she waited on her two invalids, and it seemed nothing more was needed to complete the family's happiness.

But questions were in the air that needed to be answered. Jo was seen to shake her fist at Mr. Brooke's umbrella, which had been left in the hall. Meg jumped when the bell rang and coloured when John's name was mentioned. Laurie went by the house in the afternoon and seeing Meg at the window, fell down on one knee in the snow and clasped his hands romantically. When Meg told him to behave himself and go away, he wrung imaginary tears out of his handkerchief and staggered off in mock despair.

"He's showing you how your John will go on. Touching, isn't it?" laughed Jo scornfully.

"Don't say *my John*. And please don't tease me, Jo." Meg bent over her sewing with a queer little smile. "I can't say anything until John speaks. And he won't, because Father told him I was too young."

"If he did speak," Jo said accusingly, "you'd cry or blush and let him have his own way instead of giving a good, decided 'No.'"

"Not at all. I should say quite calmly, 'Thank you, Mr. Brooke, you are very kind, but I agree with my father that I am too young to enter into any engagement at present. So please say no more, but let us be friends as we were.' Then I'd walk out of the room with dignity."

Meg was about to rehearse the dignified exit when a tap on the door made her fly into her seat and begin to sew as if her life depended on it.

"Good afternoon," said John Brooke shyly, "I came to get my umbrella. That is, I came to see how your father is. That is—"

"It's very well, he's in the rack, I'll get him, and tell it you're here," Jo mumbled, and having mixed her father and John's umbrella well together, she slipped out of the room to give Meg a chance to make her speech.

But the instant they were alone, Meg moved toward the door. "Pray sit down. I'll tell Mother you're here."

"Don't go," Mr. Brooke said. "Are you afraid of me, Margaret?"

Meg blushed up to the little curls on her forehead. John had never called her anything except "Miss March" before. "How can I be afraid of you when you have been so kind to Father? I only wish I could thank you for it."

"Shall I tell you how?" asked John, taking her small hand in his and looking down at her with so much love that her heart began to flutter.

"Oh, no, please don't—I'd rather not," she whispered.

"I only want to know if you can care for me a little, Meg. I love you so much."

This was the moment for the calm, cold speech, but Meg forgot every word of it. She hung her head and answered, "I don't know," so softly that John had to stoop down to catch the foolish little reply.

"I'll wait and in the meantime, could you be learning to like me? Would it be a very hard lesson?" And he took possession of her other hand.

"Not if I chose to learn, but—" In her confusion, Annie Moffat's foolish lessons in coquetry came to Meg's mind. She pulled away her hands. "But I don't choose. Please go away!" she cried.

Poor John looked as if his castle in the air had tumbled about his ears. "Do you really mean that?" he asked anxiously.

"Yes, I do," Meg murmured and walked away.

John was pale and grave now. There is no telling what might have happened next if Aunt March had not come hobbling into the parlour, unannounced.

Meg turned scarlet, and John vanished through the study door in three strides.

"Bless me, what's all this!" cried the old lady, with a rap of her cane.

"Mr. Brooke came for his umbrella," Meg began lamely—

"Umbrella, eh? Brooke? That boy's tutor? I understand now. I know all about it. Jo blurted it out by mistake one day. You haven't gone and accepted him, child?"

"Hush! He'll hear you," Meg whispered, much troubled.

"Don't care if he does. I've something to say to you, and I must free my mind at once. Do you mean to marry this—Cook? If you do, not one penny of my money ever goes to you. Remember that and be a sensible girl."

If Aunt March had begged her grand-niece to accept John Brooke, Meg probably would have declared she couldn't

"He knows *you* have rich relations. That's why he has come a-courting."

"Aunt March, how dare you say such a thing!" Meg cried. "John wouldn't marry for money any more than I would. We are willing to work and to wait. I'm not afraid of being poor, and I know I shall be happy because he loves me and—"

The old lady was very angry. "I wash my hands of you. Don't expect anything from me when you are married to your Mr. Book!" With that, she stamped out of the house and slammed the door.

Left alone, Meg stood a moment, undecided whether to laugh or cry. Before she could make up her mind, John was at her side. "I couldn't help hearing. Thank you for defending me. Then you *do* care for me a little."

"I didn't know how much until she abused you," Meg answered softly.

think of it. Upon being ordered not to like him, she replied with unusual spirit, "I shall marry whom I please, Aunt March, and you can leave your money to anyone you wish."

"Highty tighty! You're as bad as your parents. I mean my advice kindly. You're a pretty girl and the oldest. You ought to catch a rich husband and help your family."

"Father and Mother don't think so," Meg answered, feeling brave and independent. "They like John, though he is poor."

"This Rook is poor? I thought as much! So you intend to marry a man without money and go on working harder than you do now?"

"I couldn't do better if I waited half my life! John is good and wise. Everyone likes and respects him, and I'm proud to think he cares for me." Meg looked prettier than ever in her earnestness.

"And I needn't go away, but may stay and be happy?"

Here was another chance for Meg's well-planned speech and dignified exit. Instead she hid her face in his waistcoat and whispered, "Yes, John."

Fifteen minutes later, Jo came downstairs, paused at the parlour door, and hearing no sound, nodded with satisfaction. "She has sent him away and that affair is settled!" She opened the door prepared to praise her strong-minded sister and crow over a fallen enemy. It was certainly a shock to behold the enemy sitting on the sofa with the strong-minded sister on his knee!

Jo gave a gasp. Meg jumped up shyly. But "that man," as Jo called him, coolly crossed the room and kissed the astonished newcomer, saying, "Sister Jo, congratulate us!"

Jo rushed out of the room and up the stairs to her parents. "Do go down quickly!" she exclaimed tragically. "John Brooke is acting dreadfully, and Meg likes it!"

Mr. and Mrs. March did go down to the parlour, and a great deal of quiet talking and planning was done. Jo got little comfort from Beth and Amy when she told them the awful news, so she went up to her refuge in the garret and poured out her troubles to Scrabble and his friends.

The tea bell brought her down at last, and John and Meg looked so happy that she hadn't the heart to show how dismal she felt.

"You can't say nothing pleasant ever happens to you now, Meg," said Amy, who was charmed by the romance.

Mrs. March answered for her daughter. "The joys come close upon the sorrows.

In most families there comes now and then a year full of events. This has been such a one for us, but it ends happily after all."

"Hope the next will end better," mumbled Jo.

"I hope the third will end better still," said John, smiling at his Meg.

"Three years is a long time to wait," Amy sighed, for she would have liked a wedding in the family at once.

Just then Laurie came prancing in with a bridal-looking bouquet for "Mrs. John Brooke." "I knew John would have his way," he said, acting as if he thought he had made the match.

After a moment he drew Jo to the corner by the window. "You don't look festive," he said gently.

"It can never be the same. I just can't give Meg up," mourned Jo.

The boy put his hand on her shoulder. "You don't give her up. You only go halves," consoled Laurie. "And you've got me anyhow. I'm not good for much, I know. But I'll stand by you, Jo, for all the days of my life." And Laurie meant what he said.

CHAPTER 16

How It All Turned Out

"DON'T you wish you could look into the future and see what's going to happen to us all?" Laurie asked.

Jo shook her head. "Everyone is so happy now, I don't believe they could be much improved. And I might see something sad."

But pilgrims cannot stay long in the Pleasant Meadow, and like Christian, the March girls soon picked up their bundles and set out on the road again. It was not an easy road, and as Jo had feared, it led through some sadness; yet surprising new vistas appeared quite as fair as the air castles dreamed up when they were all young.

The three years before Meg's marriage passed quickly. John Brooke spent a year on the battlefields with the Union Army,

was wounded and sent home. As soon as he recovered his health, he set about finding work and earning money to make a home for his bride. It was Laurie, now a dashing college man, who named their little brown house the "Dovecote," for he said that Meg and John went about building like a pair of turtledoves.

By the time of the wedding, the Dovecote was ready to the last duster and dishcloth hemmed by Beth, and the different coloured soaps to match the different rooms arranged by Amy. It was not a fine mansion such as Sallie Gardiner came to when she married Ned Moffat, but everyone felt that there would be as much happiness in the little house as in the big one—more, perhaps, because so much loving care had gone into the making.

Even Jo had to admit that if one must have a wedding, Meg's was perfect. The parlour of the March home was decorated with garlands. Meg made her white muslin dress herself, and the only ornaments she wore were lilies of the valley, John's favourite flower. The bride horrified Aunt March by tying John's cravat in the parlour and then by greeting her guests at the porch door. "What is the world coming to?" the old lady said.

There was no bridal procession. When Aunt and Uncle Carrol and the cousins, Laurie and Mr. Laurence, and a few other friends were seated in the parlour, Mr. March and the young couple took their places under the green-garlanded arch. The sisters and their mother drew close.

All three girls wore suits of thin silvery grey, with pink roses in their hair. Jo's curly crop had lengthened into a thick coil. At nineteen her boyish angles had softened, and she carried herself with ease. Beth had grown slender and pale. Though she seldom complained and always spoke hopefully of getting better soon, the shadow of her illness never quite left her beautiful eyes. Amy, though she was only sixteen, had the bearing and grace of a full-grown woman. Her nose still afflicted her because it never *would* grow Grecian, but she consoled herself with her fair complexion, keen blue eyes, and golden curls.

"That is the prettiest wedding I've been to for an age, Ned," Sallie Moffat observed, as they drove away in their carriage. "And not a bit of style about it."

The only bridal journey Meg had was the quiet walk with John from her old home to the new. But it was nevertheless a new world into which she entered. She had her ups and downs of housekeeping as a poor man's wife, but she was too happy to envy Sallie's fine clothes and her servants and idle days. When the first year rolled around, twin babies were born—a girl and a boy—who soon became great favourites with all the Marches.

Jo never went back to Aunt March. The truth was that the old lady preferred Amy's tactful ways to Jo's blunt honesty. Amy was one of those fortunate people who enjoyed being liked and didn't mind going out of her way to give small pleasures. But she had a great weakness—money, position, fashionable accomplishments, and elegant manners were over-important in her eyes. She had yet to learn that money and rank do not confer nobility.

Jo's passion for independence had grown, and she was sure that in her writing she held the key to making her air castle come true. The garret saw more and more of her, as she worked on her novel or turned out romances for the weekly newspapers. At last she had a real success when a letter arrived from an editor who had offered a prize of a hundred dollars for a romantic tale. A prouder young woman was seldom seen, for, on opening the letter, a check for the prize money fell into her lap.

This check sent Beth and her mother to the seashore. Other checks followed in time. "The Duke's Daughter" paid the butcher's bill; "A Phantom's Hand" put down a new carpet on the parlour floor; "The Curse of the Coventrys" provided the family with groceries. But money to help in the household was only a part of Jo's air castle. She wanted the satisfaction and fame of serious authorship, too. So she worked hard and finished her novel and actually found a publisher for it—provided she cut it down one-third and took out all the parts she most admired.

"Don't spoil your book," her father advised in his unworldly fashion. But her mother thought it would be helpful to have the story read by outsiders. Beth decided the question by saying with a wistful smile, "I should like to see it printed *soon*." When the book came out, it met with as much blame as praise, and Jo needed all the comfort her family and Laurie could bestow to bear the trials of being "an authoress."

Poor Jo had another disappointment at this time which was even harder to bear. The Carrols were going to Europe for a year, and Aunt March arranged to send one of her grandnieces along. Jo had always longed to travel abroad, to see with her own eyes the wonders of Paris and London and Rome that she had read about so hungrily. But it was Amy who received the invitation. Jo bore up until the day the Laurence carriage rolled away to take Amy to the ship. Then she retired to the garret and cried until she couldn't cry any more.

Amy had been in raptures at her good fortune, but now that the time for leaving was at hand, she realized how far away she was going and for how long a time. She clung to Laurie at the dock, saying with a sob, "Oh, take care of them for me, and if anything should happen—"

"If anything happens, I'll come and comfort you," whispered Laurie, little dreaming that he would be called on to keep his word.

Laurie's devotion to each one of the March girls had never wavered, but, for Jo, his feelings were more than brotherly. Jo would stand for "no nonsense," however, and cut him short whenever he tried to express his feelings. She decided to go away for a while, hoping that he would fasten his affection on someone more suitable. "Beth would be just right for him," she said to herself. "If I went away, he might find it out!" And forthwith she won her parents' permission to take a job in New York as governess to the children of her mother's old friend, Mrs. Kirke.

She was soon installed on the top floor of Mrs. Kirke's boarding house. Her letters home were bright and cheerful, but Jo spent many lonely hours that winter.

She would have been lonelier still but for the friendship of one of Mrs. Kirke's boarders—a wise, bumbling, kindly professor of German. Professor Bhaer lived with his two young, motherless nephews in the big room next to her own. In Germany he had been a well-known and honoured scholar. Here in New York he was just one of many struggling foreigners, barely making enough to live on. But poor as he was, Friedrich Bhaer had within himself such richness of mind and spirit, such humour and gaiety, that everyone loved him.

Jo spent many pleasant hours with the professor, exploring the great city in company with her young charges and his nephews, and discovering the whole world

of German literature and music. His good talk about books made her realize the responsibility of a writer. She became painfully aware of the harm done to young people by the kind of lurid stories she was selling, and resolved to lay aside her writing until she could make more worthy use of her talent.

Grateful for the professor's help and friendship, Jo did not guess until long afterward what she gave in return. At forty, the professor was still unmarried, for it had never before been his fortune to find a girl like Jo. He hesitated to speak of his affection, hesitated even to hope, after something Jo said on the last day of her stay in New York.

"You must come and see us, if you travel our way," she urged warmly. "I want my family to know my new friend."

"Do you? Shall I come?" he asked eagerly.

"Yes, come next month. Laurie graduates from college then. You will enjoy an American commencement."

The eagerness disappeared from the professor's voice. "Laurie? That is your best friend of whom you speak?"

"Yes, my boy. I'm very proud of him. You'll come?"

The good man shook his head. "She is not for me, I must not hope it now," he said to himself sorrowfully. But aloud, to Jo, he only said, "I wish the friend much success and you, all happiness. God bless you," he added, and turned away.

In the winter that Jo was gone, Laurie had applied himself soberly to his studies, determined that when he graduated she should be proud of him. And she *was* proud and happy in his companionship again. But Laurie was not ready to play the brotherly role as before.

"It's no good, Jo," he said. "We've got to have it out. I've loved you ever since I've known you. I've tried to show it, but you wouldn't let me. Now I'm going to make you hear and give me an answer. Don't disappoint us—my grandfather and Beth and everyone expects us—I know that I'm not half good enough—"

"Yes, you are!" cried Jo, finding it a good deal harder to refuse Laurie than she had expected.

But she did refuse, for the love she felt for the dark-eyed, handsome boy was not that of a wife. Sorrowfully she saw him leave with his grandfather for the year in Europe they had talked about so often.

Jo had little time to regret her decision though, for Beth claimed all her attention now. When Jo came home from New York, she had been struck by the change in the gentle girl, and an unspoken fear had clutched her heart. Beth seemed to have a secret that Jo guessed but refused to put a name to. She waited for her sister to speak, waited and watched as Beth grew paler and quieter. Finally in midsummer Jo took her to the seashore once more. Perhaps by the ocean, strength and health would return.

One day as they rested on the rocky beach, Beth reached out her feeble hand and touched Jo's strong, brown cheek. The concern in the older girl's eyes was too plain to ignore. "Jo, dear, I'm glad you know," Beth murmured. "I've tried hard to tell you that I will never get well. I've known since last autumn. Don't be troubled, dear. It's best, indeed it is."

Jo held her fast as the bitter wave of this great sorrow broke over them together.

"I won't give you up!" cried Jo rebelliously. "You *must* get well."

But Beth answered quietly, "It's like the tide, Jo. When it turns, it goes slowly, but it can't be stopped. You'll tell them, when we go home?"

"What will we do without you?" Jo sobbed.

"Meg has John and the babies, but you must stand by Father and Mother, won't you, Jo? And Amy—dear little girl—I hope I shall see her again."

"She's coming next spring, and I mean to have you well by that time," Jo began. But Beth stopped her. "Jo, dear, don't hope any more. It won't do any good. Let us have happy times while we wait. I think the tide will go out easily if you help me."

Somehow the family found courage to give Beth this last wish. The months that followed *were* made happy, though the shadow of death was upon them. The pleasantest room in the house was set aside for Beth, and in it was gathered everything she most loved—flowers, pictures, her piano, the little work table, and the latest batch of beloved kittens. Amy's letters and sketches from London and Paris and Switzerland and Italy lay at hand. Jo deserted the garret and did her writing at Beth's side, and every day Meg brought the babies to be admired by "Aunty Beth." As she had hoped "the tide went out easily." The end came naturally and simply as sleep in the early spring just as the birds began to return.

To be brave and cheerful for Beth's sake had not been hard while she was with them, but the weeks and months following her sister's death were, for Jo, dark days indeed. If Laurie had been on hand and had asked again for her love, it is hard to say what answer she might have given. Neither he nor Amy had been told the whole truth about Beth's illness. Nor had Jo confided in Amy the reason for Laurie's hurried departure to Europe. Some things are hard to write when there is an ocean between.

Laurie had visited Amy in Italy at Christmas time and had been a pleasant enough dancing partner, but Amy was dismayed by the change in him. Wrapped up in her own affairs, she was slow to discover the reason for the boy's low spirits. Of her own problems, she had written home very frankly. Fred Vaughn, an English friend of the Laurences, had called on her in London and then had appeared again in Italy. He was attractive and rich and could give her all the things she thought she wanted. She was not in love with Fred, but if he asked her to marry him when he returned in the spring, she intended to say yes. She had given up the hope of becoming a great artist and meant to be an ornament of society if she got the chance.

Laurie questioned her about Fred with brotherly concern.

"He's rich and has delightful manners," Amy answered. "And I could be fond of him if I tried."

"I understand," Laurie observed lazily. "Queens of society can't get on without money. But I would not have expected this from one of your mother's girls."

These words ruffled Amy, and she turned on Laurie with a rare show of temper. It was not until she had scolded him roundly for his own aimless life that she stumbled on the reason for his discouragement. "I'm sorry," Amy said, "but I can't help wishing that you'd bear your disappointment better. Why don't you do something splendid and *make* Jo love you? If not that, then learn to forget."

The frank words on both sides rankled; but truth had been spoken in that little quarrel and when they were apart again, both Amy and Laurie were honest enough to admit it. Fred did return and ask Amy to marry him. Without regret, she sent him away. Meanwhile, Laurie had taken Amy's advice and tried to do something "splendid" with his music. He spent the winter in Vienna composing a tragic piece that was intended to stir Jo's soul. But somehow, Amy's pretty face and her new charm came between him and his tragic "Requiem." He found himself composing a sprightly opera instead, with a golden-haired heroine in a white dress and silver

At home Jo remained in the Slough of Despond. Even her writing brought no comfort, and except for one poem about Beth, no words came from her pen. The verses were not very good, but they came from a full heart. More from habit than anything else, she had sent them to a New York newspaper that printed a good deal of poetry. Though the poem was signed only with her initials, one loving pair of eyes recognized that the sorrowful lines were hers and that she was troubled.

On the very evening that Amy and Laurie returned with their tremendous news—for the marriage had been kept as a surprise—while all the family were gathered to admire and wonder, there came a knock on the Marches' door. Jo opened it, and Professor Bhaer stood beaming at her from the darkness.

If the good man had any doubt about his welcome, a look at Jo's face dispelled it as she drew him into the family circle.

bangles. He had thought the task of forgetting his "hopeless love" would take years. To his surprise he found it growing easier every day. Then came the short, grief-stricken note from Jo telling of Beth's death. His first thought was for Amy, so far from her family in this sorrow. He deserted his music and went to her at once in Switzerland.

Amy clung to Laurie and her need of him brought out a strength and manliness that Jo's independence had never done. Amy no longer scolded Laurie, and in the days that followed did everything to please him, for she found that her fondness for the boy next door had ripened into a warm, sweet love. When the Carrols decided to extend their stay in Europe, Laurie and Amy were quietly married in Paris, and with old Mr. Laurence set out on the homeward journey.

The professor's visit lasted a fortnight. When he realized that Laurie was no longer "Jo's boy," it gave him courage to ask one day as they walked together in the rain, "Can you find a little place in your heart for poor, old Fritz?"

"Oh, yes!" cried Jo immediately. "And I'm *glad* you're poor, for I couldn't bear to marry a rich man," she added, never caring whether she was proper or not as she kissed her professor under the umbrella.

"I'm to carry my share and help earn the home," she explained later to her family, "while Fritz teaches at the college out West. We love one another, and that will make waiting easier."

But the wait was not as long as they had expected. Aunt March died suddenly the following year, and in her will left Plumfield, the large old country home of the March family, to Jo.

"You'll sell the place, of course, and then you'll have enough to marry your professor," said Laurie, as they all sat talking of Jo's good fortune.

"Not at all!" Jo replied. "Fritz and I shall open a school for boys—for rich and poor, for strong and lame, for white and black—a good, happy, homelike school. Bless Fritz's dear heart; he's been helping poor boys all his life. With my professor and Father to teach them and myself to romp with them and scold them and pet them and all of you to stand by and give us sage advice—I'm sure we can do it."

"Of course you can," Meg agreed.

"It's a splendid idea, and just like Jo to think of it," added Amy warmly.

Mrs. March pressed her husband's hand and said softly, "How happy I am that the last of our little women has found her purpose in life."